MEN OF SIEGE BOOK THREE

TORREZ

BEX DANE

All my love,
Bex Dane

Published by Larken Romance

First Edition June 2019

Cover by Elizabeth Mackey Designs

Torrez (Men of Siege Book Three)

Torrez the bull.

A beast in bed.

An ass in real life.

Soraya

When Torrez walked into the palace, I couldn't stop staring.

Tall, confident, sexy. And those gorgeous eyes...

So when I had the chance, I risked it all and spent one glorious night with him.

I wanted him to be my hero.

Instead I messed with the bull and got the horns.

Right through my heart.

Torrez

I called Soraya a cheater and left her broken.

Biggest mistake of my life.

She was my dream girl. I just didn't see it.

To make it right, I'll have to use all my SEAL training to help her escape.

Running for our lives isn't the best way to start a relationship, but if we survive, it'll all be worth it.

Because she'll be mine.

Torrez is a standalone novel in the Men of Siege series. If you like enemies to lovers and crazy fun road trips, you'll love Torrez.

Looking for a weekend read? Hit the road with Torrez.

Become a VIP

———

Sign up to Bex Dane's VIP reader team and receive exclusive bonus content including;

- Free books

- Advanced Reader Copies

- Behind-the-scenes secrets no one else knows

Get all this by signing up at bexdane[1].com[2]

---

1. https://bexdane.com/

2. https://bexdane.com/

Chapter 1

Veranistaad, Central Asia

Torrez

Eight million dollars.

Six months of back-breaking work.

All of it balanced on this moment.

If Cecelia didn't show up at tonight's event, this entire project was for shit. Oh, the cool three mil the prince had just deposited in my bank account would still be mine, but Zook would go berserk and I'd lose my best worker. Not just a worker, a friend and brother. I may have given up on true love and all that jazz, but Zook believed he and Cecelia were soulmates. And I loved the kid. Couldn't let him down.

The lights dimmed. The crowd stilled. And Fasul, the short Veranistaadian man who had acted as our interpreter for this build, climbed the stairs to the stage.

"Valued guests, welcome to the evening all of Veranistaad has been waiting for. Let the celebration commence with the presentation of the bride to the groom!"

Zook stood rigid next to me, his eyes scanning the exits of the palace. A palace he and I had built for Prince Maksim Sharshinbaev, the wealthiest oil mogul in Central Asia. His net worth valued in the billions, rivaled only by the oil giants in Saudi, many of which waited in this room tonight for the arrival of the bride to the wedding celebration.

Prince Maksim, with his skin as greasy as his hair, waited on his throne, overseeing the festivities like his dad was already dead. Which he wasn't. His father, King Ivan, sat next to his son on a raised stage constructed at one end of the ballroom. King Ivan didn't look anywhere near croaking either. Maksim would have a long wait to get promoted to the big chair next to his. I chuckled thinking of Maksim's frustration with his father's longevity.

Two other men sat on gilded thrones next to Maksim. His brothers, I assumed. Pavel and Yegor.

From what I could make out of security at this gig, at least six concealed-carry guards mingled in this room. Another three outside. Not good odds against the two of us, Zook being un-skilled in close-quarters combat. The shooting range and the street fighting he learned in prison made up the extent of his experience. Hopefully it wouldn't come to that. Zook would convince her to leave, and we'd get her out quietly.

Fasul repeated his introduction in two languages besides Eng-lish before he motioned to the string quartet in the corner. They played classical music or some shit.

The girl walked out, her tiny body engulfed in the most extrav-agant, over the top wedding dress I'd ever seen. She looked like a princess whose fairy godmother was high on crack when she barfed up that spectacle of glitter and lace.

She stopped and stood beside Pavel. A young bride. Makeup and jewels couldn't hide the fact the girl was barely legal. Of course the definition of "legal" varied between Veranistaad and the States. But she looked to be sixteen tops. And terrified. Her smile fell awkwardly over teeth bared far too wide to be genuine.

When the applause died, Fasul continued. "Next, please welcome the wife of Prince Yegor Sharshinbaev, back from a long stay in America to finish her master's degree from Hale, Princess Soramina."

Zook crossed his arms and widened his stance. He glared at the stage from under the brim of his hat. As Princess Soramina stepped onto the stage, the crowd applauded and Prince Yegor beamed at her. Understandable. Princess Soramina Sharshinbaev was heart-stoppingly stunning. She made me want to smile, and I didn't even know her.

Not nearly as young as Pavel's bride. Probably in her late twenties. A scarlet dress covered in sequins hugged her womanly curves. The front dipped down in a dangerous V, revealing tempting round cleavage. Her sable hair was pulled up into a bun of woven braids at the top of her head. A royal crown surrounded the big ball like Saturn's rings. Stark black lines on her eyes and severe red lips gave her the look of a porcelain Geisha. She carried the air of sexuality of a Japanese courtesan as well. Everything about her emphasized the importance of her beauty.

Zook leaned in to whisper harshly in my ear. "That was Cecelia's roommate at Hale. She went by Soraya." Excellent. Our first sign of a link to Cecelia in six months.

As Soraya moved into position beside, and slightly behind, Yegor, her heel caught on her dress and she stumbled forward. My hands came up reflexively to catch her. Yegor flinched and stepped back. Coward. Can't offer help to your wife when she trips? Luckily, she recovered and regained her balance. Yegor sent her a warning glance and pinched her elbow in what was meant to appear supportive, but was obviously a punishment for embarrassing him. What a douchebag.

"Also back from the States after earning her master's degree, please welcome the wife of Prince Maksim Sharshinbaev, Princess Celiana."

Hell yes. If Celiana is Cecelia, we got her.

Zook turned to stone next to me. He stared down the beautiful princess as she took her place on the stage beside Maksim. She was the subtler twin of Soraya. Her hair, a lighter brown than Soraya's, was also piled on top of her head and surrounded by a gaudy crown. Cecelia's dress showed less cleavage, the color subdued hues of blue and green. All my thoughts about Soraya disappeared at the sight of Zook's girl. The reason we stood in this palace today.

And now we knew the truth. Cecelia was married.

To the most egotistical tyrant I'd ever met. And I'd worked with a bunch of the world's finest assholes. Never met a narcissist like Maksim Sharshinbaev.

As the voices and clapping quieted and the music picked up again, Cecelia made eye contact with Zook. He stared her down and she proceeded to lose her shit, her painted face twisting and melting. Maksim caught sight of her and his smile faltered. With deep furrows in his brow, he rushed Cecelia off the back of the stage.

"Fucking hell." Zook stepped toward them.

I grabbed his arm and he paused to look at me. "Take it easy."

"I can't fucking take it easy. He's going to hurt her." He spoke through gritted teeth.

"Stick to the plan. You go in now and reveal yourself, everything is shot to shit. We'll never get her out of here."

"Change in plans. We're leaving right fucking now." His muscles tensed, and his eyes tracked Maksim emerging from behind the stage, alone.

"Calm the fuck down. You go back there all fired up and cause a scene, he'll have her gone to some other palace in a split second. It'll take you another year to find her."

Soraya glanced at the unfolding events with a practiced smile plastered to her face. She stood behind the new bride, greeting guests with ease and charm. Only the few small twitches of her eyebrows gave any hint of concern for Cecelia. When Maksim returned to the stage, she didn't spare him a blink or a nod to acknowledge him.

Zook grimaced at me over his shoulder. "Fuck! You're right. Goddamn. I have no self-control right now. None."

"Go cool down. We'll gather more intel and formulate a plan to get her out."

"Fine."

Oh shit. He did not mean that at all. "You're going back there right now. Aren't you?"

"Of course. She's alone. I need to find out the truth. She doesn't love that asshole."

"We don't have enough information at this point. If you can convince her to leave, tell her we need to wait for the right moment to strike. She should sit tight and don't let anything on to Maksim."

He nodded, but it was a quick nod to get me to shut up. He had no intention to follow my advice. He strode toward the curtain that led behind the stage.

The entire ten minutes Zook spent in the back with Cecelia, I studied Soraya. She moved in a sultry way. Specifically the movement of her ass. The gown hugged her curves like a gourmet buffet. She kept a close enough distance to Yegor to say she was with him. Her smile would appear natural to the crowd, yet she held her neck and shoulders painfully stiff.

Zook returned from behind the curtain, his face red. He took a deep breath to school his features, but his labored breathing gave him away. Maksim didn't appear to notice Zook at all.

Cecelia came out next. She straightened her neck and swept her gown to the side with her hand. Graceful. Covering whatever happened between them like a seasoned con artist.

Maksim grinned and made his way over to us with Cecelia, Yegor, and Soraya in tow.

"Princess Celiana, Princess Soramina, and Prince Yegor. These are the American contractors who constructed this palace for you. Zook Guthrie and Torrez Lavonte."

It still irked me we'd used our real names, but we needed the credibility. My connections to Dubare most likely helped us win this job. Scumbags liked to stick together.

Zook and Cecelia exchanged a tension-filled nod. I met Soraya's gaze. She smiled a seductive grin, and her long dark lashes flitted down slowly, then open again.

Whoa. Did I imagine that? Was she flirting with me? Or was Yegor's wife just exceptionally friendly?

"Are you in the market for a wife?" Yegor asked me.

Oh shit. "Me? No. Not looking for a wife. Divorced."

"Ahh. If you change your mind, let me know." Yegor talked about women like a used car salesman, ulterior motives gleaming in his eyes. "We have exceptional women here as you can see." He pointed to Soraya.

Holy hell. "I see."

She tilted her chin and spread her lips slightly, her tongue sneaking out to lick the middle of her plush lower lip. Yes, clearly flirting with me. Her signal came through loud and clear, regardless of her husband standing less than two feet away.

I'd never met Yegor before and his first words to me offered me a wife? His wife?

Yegor watched as Maksim smiled and waved his hand in front of Cecelia like I could have her too if the dollars met the mark.

Something was way off here. Why would two foreign princes be interested in marrying a woman off to me? I wasn't in oil. I had a lucrative construction business and some Mafia ties that might interest them, but nothing about me would benefit them financially or socially.

"If you'll excuse me," Zook said. Oh yeah, the way Maksim motioned toward Cecelia would send him over the edge. He pivoted on his heel and walked stiffly away from the group.

"Pleasure to meet you." I nodded in the general direction of Soraya and followed Zook to the foyer.

"Fuck this shit." Zook paced in the hallway, speaking way too loud.

I stepped over to him and kept my voice low, a reminder to him to do the same. "What happened behind the stage?"

He stopped pacing and glared at me. "She sent me away. Told me to go."

Damn.

"She was terrified. Afraid we'd get caught. I need to get her alone and talk to her. She doesn't love him. Did you hear the way they talked about her?"

I did. Something was definitely off, but I couldn't put my finger on it. The royal family was either absurdly proud or beyond dysfunctional. We needed more intel before we could act. "We found her. Next we need to observe the schedules so you can get time alone with her. Hold your shit together and be smart right now."

"Smart?" He blew out a long breath. "I'll work on it." He started pacing again, his shoulders tight.

Right. Smart. Not a good word to use around Zook. "Play your role. If you can stand it, talk to Maksim more. Try acting like you're interested in a wife and see what he offers you." Maybe Maksim would offer Cecelia to Zook, and we could leave with her free and clear.

He shook his head. "I can't do that. The best I can do is not kill him in front of all these people."

I had to chuckle. Good to acknowledge your limits. "Alright. Go with that then. Don't blow our cover. Get through the party. I'll pump Soraya for info." She seemed quite pliable. "Remember, wait for the right time to strike. When they least expect it."

"I'll try." He nodded, and I sensed my warnings penetrated his haze better than earlier, but I still doubted his self-restraint in this situation.

We returned to the party and he took a place off to the side, leaning against the wall. His gaze locked on Cecelia and Maksim, who had returned to sit at their thrones on the stage. Not subtle, but luckily, Maksim was so self-absorbed, he didn't take note.

―――――

"TASTING THE LOCAL DELICACIES?" A female voice approached me from behind as I grabbed a rolled cut of beef from a buffet table.

To my left, Soraya's champagne flute sparkled in the light as she dipped it into a stream from a fountain. A quick glance around showed Yegor chatting with a group of men across the room, Maksim and Cecelia still on the stage next to Ivan.

I bit into the beef and met Soraya's gaze. Big hopeful globes of dark chocolate and caramel swirls looked back at me. I felt... pressure. Not only to get information out of her, but like she expected something of me. She was so enchantingly stunning, I wanted to give it to her too, whatever it was. Odd.

As she leaned closer, her aristocratic facade melted and a Cheshire cat smile grew on her face. "Why are you here?" She spoke under her breath.

"Built this place." She knew this already.

"But Zook's here for Cecelia, right?"

She spoke in an American accent, but I couldn't place the region. The way she said Zook didn't rhyme with book. Her vowels were exaggerated almost like a Southern belle, but this girl was the furthest thing from the South I'd ever seen. I chewed my last bite of beef as I scanned the room to make sure no one was watching us. A few eyes passed over us, but didn't stop. I swallowed the food in my mouth. Tasted good. "We can't talk here."

"It's romantic. Isn't it?" She continued to talk even though I'd told her not to. "A man chasing his woman down to make things right."

"You keep yappin', everything could go wrong in seconds." The censure in my tone made it clear she was being stupid.

That got her attention. She stepped back and her spine went straight, the smile wiped from her face. Her fingers tightened around the stem of her glass. "Shall we talk in the garden?"

I shook my head slightly. "Too many guards."

She nodded and leaned over the table, reaching for a pastry on the far end. Her backside looked bodacious covered in blood-red sequins. "Come to my bedroom." She gave me crazy eyes over her shoulder.

If she meant to be seductive, it came off as goofy and demented. Still, my dick twitched. Ballsy, kooky, and sexy always did it for me. Exactly my type. "You want me to come to your room? What about Yegor?"

She straightened and glanced at him. "He'll go out drinking with Pavel and Maksim. It is tradition. He won't return before morning."

"And the guards?"

"Only one will stay in the palace. The others will go to their homes. Oleg will sleep until his daytime shift begins."

As I had suspected, Soraya was a willing informant and readily provided valuable info. I'd text it to Zook ASAP.

"Which room is yours?"

"Second master suite on the third floor." She pinched the pastry between her thumb and forefinger and held it near her lips.

I knew where that was and how to access it. "After the party, I'll come to your room."

"How will you get in?" She shoved the pastry in her mouth, flakes sticking to her scarlet lipstick. Her fingertip pushed the bits in as she stared at me, waiting for my answer.

Couldn't hide my grin. The girl was a hot mess of naïve, funny, and aggressive. "Leave your window unlocked. Can you do that?"

"Yes." She nodded quickly. "But how will you get to my window?"

"I'm a SEAL."

Her brow scrunched together. "A marine mammal with flippers?"

My grin turned to a full smile. "No, babe. You know any marine mammals that can scale walls?"

She shook her head, still confused.

"Navy SEAL. Can handle a climb to the third floor."

Her eyes blew wide and her jaw fell slack. "Ooh." As realization set in, her head angled toward me and her hands came up slowly, like she might grip my arms to steady herself.

As before, the urge to catch her burned strong, but I kept my hands to myself. "You're cute, but cool it. Everyone's watching. We'll talk later."

"Oh, right. Sorry." She stepped back and dabbed the corners of her mouth with a folded napkin. Her face changed back to the formal air of a royal. "Speak with you later, Mr. Lavonte."

But she'd replaced her mask too late. I'd seen a glimpse of the real Soraya, and I liked her. A lot. I nodded. "Princess."

She walked into the crowd, swaying her sweet ass just for me.

Chapter 2

S oraya

He'd better not flake on me. I'd been waiting two hours for Torrez to arrive at my window and nothing. No sign of him.

At first, I'd kept my gown on and hair up, assuming he'd come right when the guests left. My heart thudded against my ribcage as I waited on the edge of my bed, staring at the open drapes and unlocked window he never came through.

Disappointed, I combed out my braids and pushed my now kinky hair back with a silver headband. I removed the gown and hung it in the closet of the new palace. The only pajamas I brought with me for the two-day trip was a long slip dress in lavender silk.

I left my makeup on. I wasn't ready for Torrez to see me without it yet.

The bed scrunched under my weight as I settled with my back against the headboard. Waiting for Torrez wracked my last nerve. Something pivotal was about to happen with Zook and Cecelia, and we needed to talk about it.

As the last guests left the party, Maksim hauled Cecelia off to an isolation room. I'd go find her first thing in the morning and make sure she had food and clothes. I wanted so badly to talk to her about Zook's arrival tonight. If he asked her to leave, would she finally be brave and do it? Could this be the catalyst she needed to give her the extra push to take the leap and jump? I didn't get a chance to ask her any of this because Maksim controlled her like he always did. Luckily, Yegor didn't connect me to Cecelia's outburst, and I wasn't punished tonight.

I noticed Zook in his cowboy hat the second I entered the ballroom. He kept his gaze riveted on the stage. I didn't know for sure why he was here, but my overactive imagination assumed he was waiting for his true love to appear so he could win her back. When she came out, I saw fireworks no one else in the room could see. My inner cheerleader went nuts, but on the outside, I kept it cool and collected. For her. I couldn't ruin her chance. Zook had come all this way to offer her one last chance, and she had to take it. She just had to.

With so much going on, now was not the time to entertain my fantasies, but sometimes the only way to cope with the overwhelming helplessness and stress of being held captive here was to escape in my head.

Tonight, a mysterious man with gleaming green eyes starred in my imaginary show.

Torrez Lavonte.

Why was he here? To help Zook win Cecelia back and get her out of this hell hole?

When Zook and Cecelia left the room, I couldn't pull my gaze off Torrez. His tuxedo jacket barely contained his extra-wide shoulders. The pants he wore hugged his crotch and stretched over his massive thighs. His posture wasn't formal like the other men. He stood with his arms crossed and his legs wide, ready to kick some ass if called upon. He looked like a take-no-shit commander, and I'd be the first one to jump on his ship if he offered.

More than the way he rocked the tuxedo captivated me. The light green of his eyes glowed like peridots against his tanned skin. Everything else about him was dark. Caramel skin, black thick lashes, a smoky shadow on his strong angled jaw, and charcoal hair shaved close to his head.

Anyway, back to my fantasy. Torrez would come into my room, see me lying in my bed and sit next to me. He'd lean over me and place one palm flat on the bed, so he'd be hovering over me. He'd tell me I was too stupendous and ravishing to be held prisoner like this. That I deserved to be free. I'd tell him Yegor would never let me go, no matter where I ran. He'd say he wasn't afraid. He was a Navy SEAL, and he'd protect me. He would kiss me, and the chains holding me down would disappear.

We'd break apart and I'd say, *All my life I'd prayed for a life raft and God sent me a luxury cruise ship.*

He'd chuckle and peel off his tuxedo jacket. We'd make earth-shattering love before we escaped into the night together. New lovers, holding hands, running with hope on the horizon.

As I dreamed, my hand passed over my navel and traveled downward. What if Torrez came to me and asked me to spread my legs for him? Would I do it? Hell yes. I wanted him from the second I saw him.

He'd kiss slowly up my leg, making me squirm against the cool sheets.

My hand tucked into my panties and rested over my clit. No, not my hand. His tongue. He'd found my hot core and pressed his slick tongue into me. I moaned his name, imagining him eating me, bringing me pleasure with his velvet lips.

"Soraya." His raspy whisper sounded like it was right here.

I ignored it, spread my legs wider, and arched my back, pretending Torrez had come to my room, crawled in my bed, and whispered my name.

"You thinking of me?"

There it was again. Definitely not part of my fantasy. My eyes flashed open and there, at the end of my bed, kneeled the real-life Torrez. In the moonlight, I could only make out his outline. The big round head, the gigantic shoulders.

Oh god, he caught me touching myself.

Humiliation rushed through me. I sat up straight and coughed. "Uh..."

Oh my goodness. What had I done? Embarrassed myself in front of the sexiest man alive?

"You were thinking of me. You said my name." He didn't move, his voice as coarse as sandpaper. The energy coming off him hit me like a hot blast of air from an oven.

I gulped down the lump in my throat and attempted to form words. What could a girl say when the object of her fantasy caught her on the cusp of masturbation? "I was uh, just waiting for you."

He moved slowly forward, like a chameleon about to snatch up a cricket. "You were imagining me touching you."

"Um..." It was totally true. He'd caught me. I couldn't deny it. "Yes."

The heat of his hand wrapped around the top of my foot, pulling a gasp from deep in my throat. He dragged my leg wider, and I let him. The way his eyes fixated on me and his attention commanded me, I couldn't say no.

"You think of other men when you get yourself off? Not your husband?"

Oh. He wanted to embarrass me? Shame me? Fine. Two could play that way. I spread my other foot wide. "Yes. I dream of hot strangers like you, Torrez."

He grunted and prowled up on the bed. I had plenty of time to say no, but I chose not to. He'd lit a flame in me, and I didn't want it to go out.

"What did you dream? Did I kiss you here?" The scruff of his jaw and soft lips skimmed the sensitive skin behind my knee.

The buzz from his touch radiated from my knee to my core and up to my throat. "Mmm."

His hands skimmed up the insides of my spread thighs, and his hulking form crept over my body. "Did I touch parts of you your husband doesn't even know exist?"

He lowered himself and kissed me softly. I couldn't breathe. He was kissing me. Torrez Lavonte was kissing me in real life. And I loved it. His lips worked mine slowly and confidently, coaxing me to open for him.

When our tongues touched, the flame inside me exploded into a blazing inferno. He must've felt it too because he moaned into my mouth and notched up the urgency of the kiss.

My hands grabbed his back. I felt his dress shirt so he must've already taken off his jacket.

"Did I dive into your sweet pussy?"

Holy crap. Was this happening?

He kissed down my chest and belly, stopping at the apex of my legs. He hovered over my sex, his hot breath washing over me like a kiss.

"Oh god!" I arched my back more, aching to get his mouth on me.

"What do you want, Princess Soraya? You want Torrez to suck your clit?"

Still in shock, caught up in the fantasy, I blurted, "Yes!"

His hands gripped my ass and squeezed. "Fuck, you got a beautiful ass. Wrap my hands around that fucker and got some meat to hold on to. Perfectly round. Does your husband enjoy your ass?"

"No... ugh..." I could barely talk. He had me riding a thin wire.

"He should partake of your ass. He's missing out. If you were my wife, your ass would be well utilized. You'd have trouble walking around the palace in your princess shoes and your princess garb because your ass would be sore every damn day."

"Argh!" This was torture. His talk was driving me wild.

"You like that idea, don't you? You want your ass fucked. My big cock up your ass. You'd love it. Fill you up. Make you come so hard you'd never forget me."

He worked my underwear down and off before his big strong hands returned to my butt, squeezing and massaging. So good. He pulled the cheeks apart and slid a finger down the crack.

I gasped and writhed in his firm hold.

"Aww, shit. You've never been touched there, have you? A virgin ass. My favorite thing. Takes time to prepare a virgin ass. Time and lube. Both of which we don't have. So I'm gonna save that for another day."

Another day? We'd have more time together? His finger slid around from behind and teased my wetness. I dropped my hands to his head and pushed. His hair was softer than it looked. His scalp was hot as hell and firm like a bowling ball.

He resisted my force, and kept his mouth hovering over me but not quite touching. He still had his clothes on, but I felt more intimate with him than I ever had with anyone else.

"We got plenty of lube here." He bent down and swiped his tongue over my slit from bottom to top as his fingers slid inside me. He grazed my clit and I squealed. "Quiet, princess. We get caught and all the fun is over. We'll both end up in a ditch somewhere with a Sharshinbaev sword through our guts."

"No. Please. Yes..." I was an incoherent blob of goo for Torrez. He could say anything, do anything, just please touch me there again. I felt so tiny in his hands. And so sexy. I was a different creature than I'd ever been. I was new.

He swiped his tongue again from bottom to top. My hips rose from the bed, trying to get him to stay longer.

"What do you want, princess?"

"I want you to shut the fuck up and eat me, Torrez! Eat me raw, you goddamn fucker."

"Shh..." He snickered as he shushed me. "The princess has a mouth like a sailor."

I opened my mouth to yell at him more, but he finally pressed his lips to my sex and started moving. He nipped and kissed and his tongue did magic circles as his fingers worked inside me. The pleasure sizzled in every cell of my body. I grunted loud, and he reached a hand up to cover my mouth. Shoot. Right. Don't want to get killed for this.

He drove me to the edge with his hot mouth, teasing me in the most excruciating way.

"You close, baby? I can tell you're close."

"Mmm." My agreement garbled under his big palm covering my mouth.

"Suck my finger and I'll make you come. Don't stop sucking or you'll make too much noise."

I nodded. He released my mouth and wiggled two fingers at my lips. I sucked them in. His fingers were big and rough and tasted sweet from my juices. God, this was hot. His head went back down between my legs. His tongue drilled in on my clit, and I couldn't hold it back. An orgasm so strong rose from my feet and surged through my body. I floated above the bed in a daze of hot pulses, wet tongue, and Torrez' fingers in my mouth. Heaven.

By the time I came back to reality, Torrez hovered naked on top of me. "Gonna fuck you now. Wearing a glove. Don't worry."

Thank god. I vaguely nodded but couldn't form words to tell him I was on the pill. The urgency of the need to have him inside me muted my brain.

A giant cock found the groove of my opening, and his hot breath hit my ear as he lay down over me. I was engulfed in Torrez. I grasped his huge shoulders and wrapped my legs around his hips.

"You ready, princess? You gonna take my big cock?"

I nodded. Yes! Yes!

"Gotta kiss you to keep you quiet, 'cuz you're gonna wanna scream again when you feel me piercing you with this thing."

Rough lips crashed down on my mouth. I answered back, loving every second of it. It all felt too good. Too good to be true. No man could be this hot in the bedroom. It couldn't be possible that he said things he was saying. Things I didn't even know I wanted to hear until he said them. Wrong, bad things, but oh so right. Right now, all his words set me on fire.

I tilted my hips and the tip of his cock stretched me wide. He moaned into my mouth as he worked his way inside. Inch by inch, he sank deeper into me. He broke the kiss and nuzzled my cheek. "Fuck, baby. Fuck me. So good. So tight. Fucking hell."

His gruff words in my ear dragged me deeper into the sensual miasma. As he started to move, his groin rubbed my sensitive clit. My hips answered back until we found a sweet spot where we both received mutual pleasure. Two bodies connecting.

I grunted and he moved his mouth back over mine. His tongue probed deep, his cock slammed into me, my clit tingled with every delicious stroke.

Another orgasm pushed through me, and I gasped into his mouth. My walls contracted around him and he lost control. His kiss became messy, his thrusts fast and uneven like a pumping oil rig spinning out of control.

When I thought I couldn't handle any more, he tensed. His arms around me tightened, and he planted himself deep. He groaned into my neck and grunted as he found his release.

Yes! Yes!

I did this to him. I made him come like that. We exploded together like dynamite, both of us lost in the spectacular heat of the moment.

He collapsed on top of me and kissed my neck. "Fuuuuck."

"Mmm."

His hands pushed my hair away from my face and his body relaxed. I rubbed his back and ran my fingers through all the sinewy muscles and ridges there. Torrez Lavonte was an awe-inspiring specimen of a man.

"Staying here a minute," he mumbled as he pulled out and settled next to me with his arm and leg still crossing my body.

"Mmm." Stay forever. Stay like this forever.

Chapter 3

―――――

I woke facing a sleeping bull. Torrez naked, at rest, with his eyes closed was a vision. A face you'd love to see every morning for the rest of your life. Over the sheet, his hand rested possessively on my hip.

Like I was his.

The weight of his arm and the warmth of his fingers grounded me, made me feel safe.

Protected.

The dawn light through the window shined on his caramel skin and his... tattoos. Oh my, so many tattoos. He was covered in green and black and red. Names over his heart, a skeleton frog between his massive pecs, a Brazilian flag on his lats, an eagle and trident on his bicep. On his left pec, a fierce bull ready to charge. Ha! I knew he was a raging bull. But below that, a Texas star wrapped up in a purple lupine. Gentle and sweet. My fingers caressed the bull. His eyes opened.

"Hey." He tugged my hip. His other hand slid under my neck and pulled my head closer to his. He kissed me casually, like it was our way. Soft and smooth. "Mornin'." His deep voice rasped as he cleared his throat.

My stomach dipped in the best way. All the embarrassment of being caught touching myself evaporated after what we'd shared. He made me feel so accepted and unconditionally sexy, like I could do anything in front of him and not worry about being judged.

"Morning." I smiled as he kissed me again, nice and smooth. So good. I wanted him. Something in this man called to me. We could be phenomenal together. Storm the world.

He deepened the kiss. Yes! My hand slid from his bicep, down his narrow waist, and gripped his hard dick through the sheet. So big. Memories of it stretching me open flooded my brain and sent a gush of heat through me. "Morning wood?"

"Morning's got nothing to do with it. That's all you."

"Mmm." I squeezed his dick, and he moaned as he moved over me.

Very subtly, he glanced at his watch. My clock said five in the morning. Had we only slept an hour together? It felt like longer but was over in a flash.

"When do you expect your husband back?"

He probably didn't intend to be mean, but the word *husband* made me cringe. I hated it but the truth hurt. I had a husband, and I was in bed with another man. Every pore of my skin loathed Yegor and this stupid marriage in name only. I didn't choose it. He and Ivan forced me to stay and comply.

A pang of remorse stung my belly. Torrez would leave soon, and I'd be alone again. My temporary escape would be over. If only Torrez were here to set me free, like my fantasy. But wait...

Part of my fantasy came true last night. Why couldn't the rest happen too? If Zook was here for Cecelia, Torrez could be here for me. Right?

"We have some time before he gets back, but we should talk." I let my hands explore his back, following the curve of his spine to his ass. I squeezed the firm round rocks.

He growled. "Yes. Shit. I'm sorry about last night. We were supposed to talk. But you looked so tempting in your bed, waiting for me, saying my name. I took advantage... Couldn't resist. You're so goddamn sexy."

My heart swelled at his compliment. He felt the same things I did. "It's okay. I wanted it too. I loved it."

He grinned and pressed a kiss to my lips. A vibrating buzz from the nightstand next to the bed caused his forehead to crinkle. His long arm stretched over my chest and picked up his phone.

"What the fuck?" His tone turned to instantly furious. "There a reason you can't stick to the plan?"

The plan? He must be talking to Zook. The plan we were supposed to talk about and didn't get to.

In my mind, the plan was to get Cecelia and me out of the country. Torrez and I would fall in love, settle down in the States, and he'd protect me from Yegor.

My hero stood and his naked ass distracted me. And more ink. Extensive tattoos on his back. My eyes didn't know where to focus. On his round butt as he pulled on his boxer briefs or those colorful tattoos, trying to figure out what they were. His sleek skin shined like someone had rubbed a rich coat of lotion over it.

"And is she ready to run?" he asked who I assumed to be Zook.

Was Cecelia ready to run? She was always too afraid. Would Zook coming here be enough to convince her? I hoped so. "Good to hear. Makes all this bullshit worth it."

Yay! She was leaving with Zook, and I was leaving with Torrez! I sat up in the bed and watched Torrez pull on his tuxedo pants and shirt.

"Sure." He sounded uncertain as he did up the buttons of his shirt. "Meet me in the garage in fifteen minutes. I'll have a car."

Fifteen minutes? We had to hurry!

I scrambled out of the bed and grabbed the closest item of clothing from my closet. The sheer dress I slipped over my head showed my nipples, but it was all I had for the moment and I was confused.

He dropped his phone in his pocket and lifted a gun off the side table. He checked it before tucking it behind his back. A gun? How come I never saw it or felt it? When did he take it off? Was he wearing that when he ate me out a few hours ago?

His eyes fell on me for the first time since he got out of bed. His whole demeanor had changed. The bright green in his eyes had dulled. No softness in his face, no sexy man. He was all Navy

SEAL ready to take care of business. How lucky were Cecelia and I to have these two guys to help us escape?

Doubt crept into my mind. Torrez *was* here for me, right? We hadn't had time to talk yet, but he wouldn't come for Cecelia and leave me behind, would he?

"I have to go now." Torrez stood by the open window and slipped his arms into his jacket.

"What?"

"We're leaving early. Bye, princess." He propped one leg over the window sill.

Leaving? "Wait. Wait. Come back. What about me? Aren't you taking me with you?" He froze with his shoulders hunched in the window frame, one foot out on the roof. "Take me with you."

He swung his leg back over and stood by the window, staring at me. His eyes scanned my dress and my obvious nipples and moved back to my face. "You want to leave him?"

Why was he asking this? Didn't he understand? We talked about it, right? "Of course. I've always wanted it." I guess we didn't discuss it. Darn. Why did I let the passion overtake me and not talk to him first? My stupid fantasies would get me killed one day.

"Listen. I'm sorry if you're in a shitty situation with your husband, but I'm not your ticket outta here." His voice created a vast distance between us.

My ticket out? Where did he get that idea? The spoiled princess in me reared her head and spat out something I didn't mean to say. "An honorable man would take me with him."

Now I didn't know this man well, but anyone could read his face. The deep furrow growing in his forehead, his nostrils flaring, his green eyes turning dark emerald.

His flat palm came up and pushed the air, like he was trying to ward off evil. "What do you know about honor? You ever fought in combat? You ever carried a dead brother through a hailstorm of bullets? You ever given up your dreams for someone you love? You know shit about honor. You've been hiding here in your palace where champagne flows from spigots. Don't talk to me about honor."

Oh shoot. I said the wrong thing. I didn't mean to question his honor. Darn. Darn. This was going from awful to catastrophic fast.

He huffed a short breath and pulled his shoulders back. The pain left his face and stinging bitterness took its place. I felt like the matador about to be scored by the sharp horns of an enraged bull. Finally, he spoke. "You set me up."

Set him up? "What? No. I didn't..."

"You set this whole thing up. How did I not see it? You want out of whatever fucked up situation you're in with Yegor, and you seduced me so I'd take you on."

Oh my god, no. He thought I had planned this? I thought *he* planned this. "Zook's here to rescue Cecelia and you're here to rescue me, right? I mean, you have a gun and everything." It sounded pathetic when I said it out loud.

"No." He spoke slowly, like I was stupid. "I have a weapon to provide backup for Zook. I didn't even know you'd be here."

"But you came to my room."

"To get information about Cecelia and the security in this place." His stone cold voice hit me like a smack. "The mission is extract Cecelia. Zook wasn't sure she'd be there last night, but she was. He's convinced her to leave with him. Now I need to go take his back. *You* are not part of the mission."

Of course he wasn't here for me. He didn't even know me before last night. Why would he risk his life for a stranger? No one was ever coming for me. God, how could I be so naïve? I lost myself in a fantasy and totally misread everything.

But Torrez and I had shared so much. He must've felt it too. I couldn't have mistaken his deep passion for... "Make me part of the mission. Please."

I stepped to him and he took a step back.

"You in on it with him?" he asked me.

"In on what?"

"You and Yegor sell women." He spoke low and deadly. "You sell yourself? You're a whore?"

His words sliced sharp through my gut. He meant to hurt me. Last night it was fun. Now it cut deep into the wounds Yegor had etched into my soul. The outward physical bruises healed, but the shame scarred forever. Torrez didn't know what he was saying. No girl wants to be called a whore, but to me, it hurt so much more because Yegor had beaten me with the same words since I was seventeen. I froze and wrapped my arms around myself like Torrez had stabbed me. I made a mistake, but I didn't deserve this!

"You're a lying, cheating whore."

Oh god no. Stop. I'd triggered his attack mode. The vicious minotaur was preparing to destroy me.

"You conned me good. Had me thinking you loved my cock. I know women like you. I was married to one. You'll fuck the next guy who rounds the corner and con him too to get what you want."

"No." I dropped my head as tears flowed from my cheeks. "No." I spoke so quiet, he probably didn't even hear me.

"I'm not taking you with me, you manipulative slut. Glad I used a fucking glove last night. Who knows what stank you're carrying in that cunt."

I fell to my knees. Fire burned through me and singed me to the core. What he said wasn't true. He didn't understand. Nothing mattered. I was alone. Cecelia would be gone, and I'd be left behind with no chance of ever getting out. Even if we had time to talk, Torrez would never believe me. He'd made up his mind.

When I looked up, he was gone. Only the curtain flailed in the breeze.

———————

I WAS CRYING IN MY bed when Yegor marched in an hour later.

"Maksim is dead and Celiana is gone."

"Gone?"

"What do you know?"

"Nothing. Nothing."

"Did you hear an intruder?"

"No. Nothing."

His eyes narrowed. "Have you been crying?"

"I was emotional after the ceremony. That's all."

He stepped in and looked around my room. Luckily, I'd closed the window.

"Where did Celiana go?" His words slurred, and he smelled like alcohol.

"I don't know. I swear."

"Liar!" He slugged my cheek and my knees collapsed.

"Isolation then until you tell the truth."

Chapter 4

---

*S*oraya

My hands shook as I stepped out of the taxi. The layer of sweat on my palms squeaked between my skin and the shiny blue surface of my American passport.

An American passport for Soraya Merrington. The name I used in the States. A person who didn't exist. It didn't make any sense. My uncle, Ivan as he preferred me to refer to him, told me I was adopted as a baby from an American woman who lived here in Veranistaad. She was poor and dying from cancer when she gave me up for adoption.

Ivan said because my mother was American, I was American too. I never knew her or my father, so I couldn't ask. I didn't question Ivan. He had warned against it, and I found it too painful to ask. But every time I signed my name Soraya Merrington, I wondered if that was my name before I was adopted.

When Ivan told me I would marry his son Yegor, I cried all night. I didn't know him well because I had been away at boarding schools, but I thought of him like a brother. I ran away before the wedding. Ran to the police station in Portul. They laughed at me and called Yegor to pick me up. That was when the beatings and shaming began. Yegor warned me with each strike "Never humiliate the family again." If I served my role, I'd be granted freedom to go to school wherever I wanted. I complied because I was scared and didn't want to leave Cecelia. She promised me we would escape once we had our degrees. We'd get new identities so Ivan couldn't find us. Since we'd been back, Cecelia had been too depressed to make plans. Thank God Zook came last week and forced her to leave.

So now, ironically, I stood in front of the American Embassy with my American passport in my hands waiting to pick up my diploma from Hale University.

I felt broken and terrified. Broken because my best friend and sister had been gone a week with no word. Broken by Torrez and the scornful wrath he bestowed upon me before he escaped out my window. I'd made a horrific mistake.

And terrified because this felt wrong. Hale didn't deliver diplomas to embassies. They didn't send letters to the palace saying I must pick up my diploma in person and bring my passport. Cecelia and I graduated more than six months ago. I'd received my diploma in the mail before I left the States. So had she. And she didn't receive the letter from Hale instructing her to go on this wild goose chase of an errand I'd been sent on today.

Yegor had questioned it. He came to the isolation room I'd been in for a week and asked me to explain. I couldn't because I didn't know anything about it. He was preoccupied dealing with funeral arrangements, publicity, and the business after the fallout of Maksim's death. Yegor barely looked at me and waved his hand for me to leave the isolation room. "Take Leonid. No side trips." He gave me my passport and Leonid drove me here.

Nothing struck me as off on the street in front of the embassy. I felt Leonid's gaze on me as I scaled the steps up to the front gate. The guard sitting at the concierge desk in the vast white lobby looked up as I approached his window.

"Uh, I'm Soraya Merrington." I set my passport on the counter, hoping he didn't notice the crumpled sweaty cover. "I'm here to pick up a letter from Hale University."

He took my passport and typed into his computer. "Follow me." He stood and walked through thick double doors. My heart pounded as I followed him. The doors clicked shut, separating me from my world, locking me into another dimension.

As he led me to a small sideroom, panic rose in my throat. He motioned for me to enter and left as the door closed behind me. This wasn't right. Why wouldn't he just hand me my diploma? Why did I have to go deep into the embassy?

Inside the room, the back of a chair faced me. Tall suede work boots attached to huge legs crossed at the ankle rested on the desk. As the chair swiveled, closely shaved black hair, a killer jaw, and sparkling green eyes fixed on me.

No.

Torrez?

My stomach plummeted like an elevator disconnected from its safety cables.

He smirked at me.

The elevator smashed into the bottom floor.

Torrez came back? Why? To kill me?

I spun and grabbed the door handle. It rattled. Locked. Shit! They locked me in here with a lunatic? Holy crow.

I'm going to die.

He must've gotten out of his chair fast because his arm around my waist pulled me back before I even tried to unlock it.

The scream I let out died against the thick wooden door. The room had no windows. Only a desk and a chair. "Help!" I stretched my upper body forward and banged the door. "Help."

He lifted me up and my feet kicked in the air.

Think, Soraya. Self defense.

What weapons did I have? I bent my leg and jabbed the spike of my heel into his knee.

"Ow, fuck."

Good. I hurt him. I bent my other leg to get him again...

Whoosh!

His immense body had me pinned to the floor, my face smashed to the cool tile.

"Calm the fuck down." His mouth hovered right by my ear.

Holy crow. He's not here to kill me. He's going to rape me.

"No! Don't touch me. Help!" I struggled to get my hands underneath me but he grabbed them in his big mitts and immobilized me.

"Settle down."

"Argh!" His hands wrapped around my wrists like manacles and held mine to the floor on either side of me. I bucked my hips but he didn't budge. Heavy as a boulder. Was the man made of granite?

"I'm not gonna hurt you." I could hear the forced patience in his tone.

Fear still roiled in my stomach. "Yeah, right. You're gonna kill me or rape me."

"I am not," he spat back.

I wanted to believe him. First because I didn't want to be killed or raped, but also because the remnants of the naïve child deep inside me still held hope.

He could be here for me.

I stopped fighting and let my limbs go limp. "You're not?"

"No." He dragged out the word like it was obvious.

"Why are you here then?" I didn't want it to but darn, darn, hope reared its head and smiled.

He could be here for me.

"You done fighting so we can talk?"

Was I? I still felt like fighting but I also wanted him off me. Because Torrez Lavonte's massive body on mine felt so good. All his power and strength over me. Now that I knew I wasn't going to die or get raped, I could enjoy the feel of his hard chest on my back, his breath in my ear, his chuckle...

"Don't laugh at me."

"You're funny." He didn't lift his weight as he enjoyed a laugh at my expense.

"I am not funny." Idiot. "Get off me, you big oaf."

His chest lifted but his hands stayed tight around my wrists. "No more screaming?"

"Fine." God, get this man off me.

The rest of his weight left me, and cold air pricked my skin where his heat had been. I took in a big breath since he wasn't crushing my lungs anymore. He offered me his hand but I ignored it. Not touching him again. Ever.

I fixed my clothes and glared at him. Damn, his eyes glowed pretty in these lights. I'd forgotten how bulky he was. His dark jeans and a gunmetal gray Henley hugged all his bumps and curves. Torrez was a huge, gorgeous man. "Tell me why you're here." Crush my hopes before they take flight.

He ran his hand over his head and pierced me with those green eyes and a repentant grin. "You still want out?"

He was messing with me again. Leading me on only to crush me. "Out of what?"

"Your marriage. This place." He looked up at the ceiling, but he meant Veranistaad. Well, I wasn't giving in so easy. He'd have to work for it if he was here for me.

"What business of that is yours?"

"You told me you wanted out. Cecelia and Zook filled me in on the details of what's happening here."

"And what do you think is happening here?"

"You were forced to marry Yegor. He treats you like a slave."

The word hurt. We hadn't been called that before but that was what we were, Cecelia and I. We had freedom when we were at school, but it was all a temporary facade contingent on us ultimately coming back here and playing our roles.

"I'm not a slave."

"Do you have any freedom? Can you leave when you want?"

"Yes." I lied.

"You're lying."

"I could leave if I chose."

"Then why haven't you?"

That question drove me insane. When something is beaten into you from a young age, and your first few attempts to escape fail, getting up the courage to try again seems impossible. I had a plan. I was about to implement it when Zook showed up. Then Yegor locked me up for a week and now we were here, facing the ugly truth. I hadn't escaped yet. I was twenty-three. I'd been under Ivan and Yegor's control for thirteen years, and I had not made the giant leap to leave.

He answered for me. "Because Yegor would chase you down and beat you, shame you, kill you?"

He knew. No point in lying to him now. I nodded. Embarrassed. "I have tried to escape. He finds me and brings me back. Only so many times a girl can take a verbal and physical beating before she gives up."

His eyes softened and his head dipped. "You don't deserve that. It's not right. Leave with me. Today. He won't find you."

There it was. Torrez came for me.

"Private jet waiting at the airport. I'll take you to Boston. Protect you from him."

A tense pause stretched out between us as we stared each other down. His offer was very tempting. But he'd also treated me like shit a week ago, proving he couldn't be trusted.

"You shouldn't have come all this way." I turned away from him to create more space between us. I needed a buffer. Why did he have to be so gorgeous and such an ass? If this was all some sick kind of trick to strike me down again...

"Pardon?"

I had made it back to the door. If I unlocked it, I could make it to Leonid. Torrez might chase me, but at least I'd get out of this room. Maybe the clerk would help me or Leonid would see me running. But then Leonid would shoot Torrez, and as much as I hated him, I didn't want that. "You wasted a trip. You should've stayed in the States with Cecelia and Zook and left me here."

His brow wrinkled and he took a slow step closer to me. "I never left."

I paused with my hand on the doorknob. "What do you mean?"

"I've been here a week. Never left you, Soraya." His voice was soft and gentle.

He never left? Well that was nice. Hope sprung up again. Maybe he really was here for me. "Regardless, I can't trust you and therefore, I cannot put my life in your hands."

"Why can't you trust me?"

"Men can't be trusted. American, Veranistaadian, pretty much anyone with a cock, you can't trust."

His eyes widened. "What are you afraid I'll do to you?"

"Oh, I don't know. Disappear. Leave me standing alone in the snow. I may be treated like a slave, but at least I have shelter and food. Why would I leave with a man who thinks I'm a whore?"

He took another step toward me. "Listen..."

I held up my palm flat with my back against the door. "Stay back. Why should I trust a man who would leave me behind after he knew Maksim had been killed and Ivan would be furious Cecelia escaped?"

"When I left, it hadn't escalated to violence yet. We were gonna make a clean run for it."

"But when I told you I wanted to run with you, you turned on me. On a dime. From nowhere, I became a whore and a manipulative slut. You said you knew women like me? Well, I know men like you. I've felt their knuckles strike my cheek. I've felt the bruises in my ribs when I walk. No, I'm not leaving the safety of my home for a man like you."

He growled and his fists clenched. "I would never lay a hand on a woman." He placed his hands above my head and leaned in, towering over me. "Unless she asked me to and she'd enjoy the fuck out of it." The corner of his mouth twitched.

I stifled my reaction because what he said was funny, but I would never let him see I thought that.

He crowded me against the door. His heat and energy engulfed me. The wall of Torrez blocked my vision.

"My turn to talk. I'm sorry I called you a whore and a manipulative slut." I cringed hearing the words again. "I made a mistake. A huge one. I let my past cloud my judgement. I felt cornered and chose to cut and run. You're not a whore. I wasn't aware you were suffering here, and I regret what I said. My instincts were wrong. I knew it the second I climbed down from the roof, but it was too late. We had to get out fast. We stopped at the airport, and Zook left with Cecelia. I stayed behind and planned this way out for you."

I pushed his chest off mine and surprisingly, he moved back. "And what way is that?"

"American passport. American girl gets on a plane and flies to America. Leave your phone here so they can't track you." He pointed to the desk.

"That simple?"

"Yes."

"Yegor will come after me. He's on a rampage. He locked me in isolation for a week. He'll never give up if I run."

"That's where you need me. I'll protect you."

"How will you do that?"

He patted under his armpit through his shirt. "SEAL, remember?"

"I thought you were a marine mammal with flippers."

He chuckled. "No. A man who knows how to keep you safe from men like Yegor."

"I don't even know you."

"You know what you need to know. I did this for you. I can keep you safe. And I have a huge cock."

He did have a huge cock, but that was completely irrelevant now as I'd never see it or touch it again. "How old are you?"

"Turned thirty-eight yesterday. You?"

He spent his birthday here? Alone? "Twenty-three. You're too old for me."

His wince turned into a patronizing grin. "You got your shots in, babe. Now let's get the fuck out of here. We'll go out the back."

I took a deep breath as he stepped toward the door on the other side of the room.

"Will I see Cecelia?" I missed her so much. It might be worth it to trust Torrez just for the chance to talk to her again.

"Yes. She's safe with Zook. They know I'm making my move today."

Could it be true? Could it be this easy? Like all these years of hiding and fear could be erased if I just said yes. Inside, I heard a small voice say *yes, it could*.

"Okay."

"Okay?"

"I'll come with you. But not *with* you. I trust you enough to get me out of here. Beyond that, I want to stay with Zook and Cecelia."

"You'll be safer with me."

"You'll betray me. Like all men do."

"Not right to group all men together like that."

"Didn't you group me with all women when you left in the morning? Didn't you say you knew women like me? Whores? You were married to one?"

"I apologized for saying those things."

"You're too late. You should've taken me with you that morning, you jerk."

"I'm here now. Offering safe passage. I have a gun and everything. Say you'll come to America with me."

I looked around the room for another way out. What other choice did I have? And there was that naïve voice again.

He's here for you. "I'll go to America with you."

"Say you'll let me fuck you again." He picked up a green duffel bag from behind the desk.

Oh my god, the nerve of this man! "I will never let you touch me again, mister. Don't hold out hope for that."

Chapter 5

Torrez dropped his bag outside a door on the thirty-fourth floor of the apartment building on the West End. As he worked the key in the lock and opened the door, cold dank air—the kind of stale only months of vacancy can conjure—hit my nose.

He used his phone as a flashlight and walked inside. Tables and chairs covered in ghostly white fabric marked the edges of the room.

"I'm not staying in..."

He shushed me with his palm up as he pressed his phone to his ear. "Yo. This is Torrez Lavonte. I need the power turned on in 3401." He paused. "Right. Make sure the gas and water are on too. I'm back."

How long had he been gone? Never mind. I didn't care because Torrez would be a memory to me soon enough. I just needed him to bring me to Cecelia and this nightmare of a journey could be over.

His boots made the only noise in the place as he stepped to the window. He pulled a chord and the blinds opened, revealing an iridescent view of the Boston skyline over the Charles River.

The bright lights from the boardwalk on the shore lit up the inside of the apartment.

"Wow. Quite a view."

"It'll do." He dropped his phone on the counter and looked at me. His face drawn from traveling, his shirt wrinkled. His overwhelming intensity had morphed into a laid-back tired version of Torrez as the hours of flight had worn on. It reminded me of how tender and peaceful he looked when he slept. Nope. Not thinking of Torrez being soft and gentle. The man had said horrible things to me and even though he'd apologized, I had zero interest in anything but getting the heck away from him.

"I'm surprised you live in a place like this." Well, okay. Maybe I was a little interested in him.

"Why?" He pulled a sheet off a very plush sectional couch covered in taupe suede. Torrez had expensive taste.

"I thought you were a contractor."

"I am. Build mansions." He balled the sheet up and tossed it to the corner.

"Still. This kind of place requires more than can be earned building mansions."

"I build a lot of mansions. Zook is fast. Got a big crew."

"How big?" Shoot. I'd made the whole trip without asking any questions. I'd promised myself I would not get to know Torrez or give him any chance to get to know me. But this place was incredible, and I was surprised because it didn't fit his appearance.

"Big enough to pay for a place like this. And another place in the Hamptons. Got property in Texas too."

He had three houses? "Texas?" There I went asking questions again.

"You spent winter in Boston before?"

"Yes, several winters. Coldest months of my life."

"Right. I spend as much time in Texas as I can in the winter. You ever been there?"

"No. I just came here for school. Didn't travel."

"You should visit sometime. World class beaches. Their idea of a storm is a misty day here."

Okay, enough charming and sweet talk with Torrez. "I'd like to see Cecelia now. How far is Zook's place from here?"

"About twenty-five minutes by car."

"Take me there."

"Tonight?" He looked at his watch. "It's dinner time. Let's get something to eat first."

"Do you have a car?"

"Not at this place. Been gone four months."

He'd been gone that long? I guess that was how long it took him and Zook to build the palace. Wow. He was fast. Regardless. "Call me a taxi."

"You just got off a fourteen hour flight, and you wanna take a taxi out to the Bluffs?"

"Yes. Call me a taxi, please."

"Something wrong with this place?" He motioned to the windows with the million-dollar view. Nothing wrong with this place. In fact, I'd love to stay here, but *he* was here.

"There's no electricity."

"Where are you safer? With a Navy SEAL up on the thirty-fifth floor of a high-security building, or in a big house alone with Zook? I love the guy, but he has no real-world experience. Besides, if something went down, he'd one hundred percent protect Cecelia before you."

I hadn't thought of the risks, I just wanted to get away from Torrez and see my best friend. "I'd still like a taxi now please."

"I'll take you there tomorrow. Tonight eat and sleep."

"Are you deaf? I've asked for a taxi several times and each time you ignore me. Forgive me if I don't want to sleep here in this dark place with ghost furniture and a dizzying view. I don't want to be anywhere near you and your... body!"

A smug grin grew on his stupid face. "My body getting under your skin?"

"No."

"I think it is. I think you're thinking about my body and how it felt when you got to touch it."

My skin turned hot. Hopefully he couldn't read the physical effect he had on me. "I am not. And you know why I'm not? Because the mouth attached to your body said vile things about *my* body. And no matter how gorgeous you are, you still said them and they make me never want to be near you again."

His jaw worked and his face hardened. "And I've apologized for that. Almost a day ago and you're still holding on to it and carrying it like a flag after you won a gold medal."

"What do you mean?"

"A bigger woman would've brushed it off. If you know it's not true, it wouldn't bother you so much. But you're holding on so tight to the pain, you're making stupid decisions. You want to go out to the Bluffs right now where it's less secure, just so you can get away from the memory of me insulting you. But even if I call you a taxi, you're still gonna be simmering on it saying in your head *I don't have diseases*." His voice rose and his lips pulled tight as he feigned a female voice. "*How dare he leave me when I asked him not to. I can't believe he called me stank after I begged him to eat me raw*."

"Oh my god!" He didn't say what I thought he just said.

"It's true, isn't it? The whole week, the entire flight, you've been repeating in your head all the shit I said and sulking and muttering to yourself *it's not true*, but you don't have the confidence to convince yourself."

Okay. That hurt worse than the original stuff he said. "Screw you, you big jerk."

"You'll never get to screw my big jerk again."

"Oh? Pfft. Like I want to."

"You know you want to. You're chomping at the bit for it."

I sputtered and turned away from him. He was making my skin crawl. I wanted to scratch his eyes out. He must've been angry too because his voice resounded through the quiet room. "Zook. I'm in Boston. Yeah. Brought the package with me." He paused. "And the package is very ungrateful." He glared at me. "It wants to come stay at your place." He listened again and his brow crinkled. "Alright. I'll tell her." He put the phone back in his pocket. "Zook's in Montana with Cecelia."

"He is? They are?"

"They're layin' low out of state for a while till they get the security on the house tightened up." He popped out one knee and propped a hand on his hip.

"Oh."

"So even if I consented to your foolish idea to call a taxi, he's not there."

"I see."

"He also doesn't think you coming to stay with him is a good idea. He wants to focus on Cecelia. Agrees you'd be better off with me."

"Hmm." Well darnit.

"So, get your panties out of your crack. Let's get food. There's a place right next to the lobby downstairs. We don't even have to walk far."

Well, I was hungry and I would love some American food. "Okay.'"

"Finally I get her okay."

As we walked to the door, the lights flickered on. He chuckled. "See? Temporary."

Chapter 6

The steaming plate of spinach fettuccine in front of me smelled divine. The flat green noodles twirled on my fork, my knife skimming off the excess sauce. Torrez dug into his meat lasagne like swine on slop. Appropriate.

He sipped his beer and eyed my twirling fork. "You gonna spin that into gold or eat it?"

The pig himself was picking on my eating style? "The proper way to eat pasta is a bite-sized morsel spun artfully around a backwards fork."

His eyes didn't blink for a few seconds. "The fuck?"

"Apparently no one bothered to teach you dining manners." I sipped my Merlot and eyed him over my glass.

He shoveled in another heap of food and talked with his mouth full. "They may have and I didn't bother to learn it. Food gets in my mouth, I've succeeded."

"Yes, well, you're a success then, aren't you?"

He swallowed, rested his elbows on the table, and leaned in. "I think it's time you let this act go."

"It's not an act. I loathe you and I won't pretend otherwise."

"I saved your ass from servitude in Veranistaad." He lowered his voice, and his gaze flitted to the left and right, making sure we had privacy.

"I'm aware of that."

"And you didn't speak a word on the plane. Not even a hint of gratitude came out of those luscious lips."

Luscious lips? Was that a compliment? I made him wait for my reply by chewing slowly. The food tasted better than it smelled. Torrez might be rough around the edges, but he enjoyed fine things. I took my time swallowing and taking another sip of wine.

"Thank you." I dipped my head and tried to sound sincere.

"Oh yeah, that was genuine. You're a piece of work, you know that?"

I'm a piece of work? He's the one who pulled the Jekyll and Hyde move. "My thank you was as earnest as your apology."

"You think I was lying?" His nostrils flared.

"I don't know. When were you lying then? When you called me *stank* or when you said you didn't mean it?"

He set his fork on his plate and wiped his lips with his napkin. "I lied to you in your room in the morning. Your pussy was the sweetest I'd ever tasted. I wanted to take you again after seeing your nipples through that sheer dress. I could see every curve as if you were buck nekkid. Entranced me. Had it on my mind the whole week I was planning your extraction. Your kinda pretty doesn't grow on trees. It's distinctly yours. So staggering, it brings a man to his knees."

Oh. Hmm. Well that was flattering and surprising. "Then why'd you say all those things and leave?"

"I'm an idiot."

"Agreed."

"Not my finest moment. I spooked when you asked me to take you. Survival instincts kicked in. I've learned not to trust people over the years."

"Like your ex-wife?" His right eye winced when I mentioned her. She must've done something horrible to him.

"Yes. And fifteen years in the military. You can't trust no one but the men who have your back. Even your brothers will sometimes turn. You go into a situation blind, you ain't walking back out. We were training those fuckers, a tenuous friendship because they'd show up one day wearing a vest. They'd lead you on a journey you'd never come back from because they'd planted an IED at the end of the road. Doesn't make a man more inclined to trust anyone."

Looking back, because we didn't talk more before we had sex, I didn't know he was seasoned military, and he didn't know I wasn't in cahoots with Yegor. "I can understand how it might've looked suspicious from your perspective, but I wasn't trying to pull a fast one on you."

"I know that now. And I didn't mean what I said. Thought you were stunning. Wanted you the moment I saw you." He shook his head slowly from side to side, his tongue sneaking out to lick his lips. "Loved the way you flirted with me right in front of Yegor. Knew you were wicked ballsy then. Man, turned me right the fuck on."

Whew. The darkness in his eyes and the honesty of his tone made my face heat up and beads of sweat form at my temples. Time to change the subject. "Anyway..."

"Thinking of you waiting there for me drove me insane." He kept going. For a man who didn't talk much before he had sex with me, he spoke profusely now. "But I knew you'd get in trouble if you got caught, so I waited till the last guest left and Yegor and his brothers were well on their way. But it was worth the wait. You tasted like sweet honey dripping from a spoon. I could eat that syrup every damn day of my life and never get tired of it. You squirming and calling my name? Hot as hell."

Holy crap. I was wet between my legs just listening to Torrez talk dirty about us. His jaw dropped as he smiled, his eyes dancing as he watched me nervously adjust in my seat.

"Loved it too much. So much I knew I was hooked, and I'd risk anything to have it again."

"Oh. Um..." Wow. I had sensed intense emotion coming from him, but after he turned on me, I assumed my imagination had made it up.

"I also really liked seeing the real you. The girl who thought Zook coming for Cecelia was romantic. Watching you try to seduce me in your awkward way."

Oh my word. I didn't realize he noticed so much about me. And he liked what he saw. Torrez needed to stop talking right now, or I might have to forgive him.

"I liked that girl. This one..." He waved his fork up and down, pointing it at me. "Not so much."

And Torrez the jerk returned. So rude! What an insolent ass-hat.

"Lavonte." The deep voice of a man approaching our table halted my inner hexing of Torrez. I cleared my throat and sucked down a huge gulp of wine, trying to collect myself.

Torrez glanced at the man, but turned his gaze back to the table.

"Greco," Torrez replied coolly. The man he called Greco had slick ebony hair and wore a cheap-looking burgundy suit with a narrow charcoal tie. Dark sunglasses covered most of his face, but what I could see held wrinkles and deep pocks.

"You returned late from your trip." Greco spoke with a thick New England accent.

"Blythe didn't take care of your needs while I was gone?" Torrez withdrew his arms from the table and rested his hands on his thighs.

"She sufficed, but I prefer to deal with you." Greco did some kind of slurping hissing thing with his teeth, like he was sucking on an ice cube. "I have a large transaction I need you to process."

"Blythe can take care of that for you." Torrez kept his eyes on his plate.

"This one is ten times larger than the last one. I'd like you to handle it personally."

"My operation is slowing down. You'll need to look for another contractor."

"I clearly want you, Lavonte."

"I'm sorry I can't be your man."

Greco placed his palms flat on the table and leaned in close to Torrez. "You trying to back out of our deal?"

Torrez met his eyes, and they locked into a visual duel. "No. I'm saying I'm scaling back."

"I'm saying you're expanding."

"You don't dictate shit to me, Greco. Nothing."

Their conversation became heated so fast, I could barely follow along, but it appeared they were business associates, and Greco wanted something from Torrez he wasn't willing to give.

Greco straightened and flattened his tie. Torrez turned his gaze to me, his face a dispassionate stare.

"It's a long climb to the top of the mountain," Greco said, cryptically. Torrez didn't reply. He remained stoic and calm, his eyes on me. "But only one wrong step to plummet to your death."

Torrez smacked his napkin next to his plate and stood to face Greco, who took a small step back and grimaced for a second before he composed himself. "I'm not climbing your mountain." Torrez almost spit in his face.

Greco took another step back and smirked at Torrez. "Oh really? Since when? For a good fifteen years you've been ghosting me on the trail."

"I blaze my own trail. Made that clear from the beginning. Now if you'll excuse us." He sat back down and picked up his fork, holding it over his plate, a clear sign he expected Greco to leave.

Greco turned his steely gaze to me, and I felt a chill pass through me. This guy was not playing around. "What's your name, babydoll?"

Torrez gritted his teeth. For the first time, he let it show Greco was getting to him. I hated that nickname, but my instincts told me this was not the kind of man who would care if I told him so. "Soraya."

"Soraya." Greco raised his nose like he was smelling my name before turning his attention back to Torrez. "Lovely. Exotic. Certainly you'd like to expand your business so you have plenty of money to accommodate a woman like the beautiful Soraya."

"She's got nothing to do with it."

"Ah, but the woman has everything to do with it. Doesn't she? Or have you forgotten?"

"She's off-limits, Greco."

"Of course. I wouldn't think of it. She's yours."

"I am not his."

He ignored me, but Torrez didn't back me up either.

"Leave us now." The edge in Torrez' voice could cut through steel.

"Fine. I'll be in touch. Goodnight, Soraya." Greco tilted his chin toward me.

"Uh, night."

As Greco sauntered out of the restaurant, Torrez snapped into motion. He stood and whipped out his wallet, tossed a wad of cash on the table, and stared down at me. "We're leaving."

"I'm not done with my food yet."

"Get the fuck up." He gripped my bicep and hauled me up. My napkin fell from my lap to the floor.

"What's your problem?"

"Walk to the exit. And keep your mouth shut."

Yep, Torrez the ass had returned full force. He waited an impatient second while I grabbed my purse. He ushered us out fast, down the half a block to the apartment building, and into the lobby. He jabbed the button and tapped his foot in the elevator up to the thirty-fourth floor, looking up at the ceiling, not at me.

When the door opened, he burst through and grabbed the bags he hadn't unpacked yet. "We're not staying here."

"Why not?"

He opened a storage closet and threw several small guns and a roll of cash as big as a roll of toilet paper in his bag. "There's a high likelihood there will be a fire in this apartment tonight."

A trickle of fear dripped along my spine. "How could you know that?"

"Because arson is Greco's preferred form of persuasion."

I gasped and pointed to the door, as if Greco were standing there. "Arson? Who is that man?"

"Let's go."

"But..." He grasped my upper arm and my feet shuffled as he hauled me back out the door.

My heart beat wildly as he made a phone call while the elevator took us back down to the lobby. A cab waited for us at the curb. I climbed in first and scooted across to the far window behind the driver.

"Where to?" the cabbie asked him.

Torrez sat next to me and stared out the side window.

"Where are we going?" Panic had taken over as the trickle of fear turned into a steady flow of terror.

He turned back to me. "Fuck. I don't know."

Oh my word. "You don't?"

"No. Goddamn fuck. I don't know." He pressed his palms to his forehead like he was fighting a migraine. "Just drive!"

"Drive where, sir?"

"South. Alright? Drive south." He shook his hands, palms up, extremely frustrated with the cab driver when all he did was ask a simple question.

"Will do." The cabbie took off.

"South? We're just going south? Like south of the city?" My hands were shaking now as the panic flooded me. If he didn't know where we were going, who did?

"I don't know," he replied more softly, turning to stare out the window again.

"I don't go south of Milton." The cabbie peered at him in the rearview with doubtful eyes.

"Fine. Take us to Milton."

"What the hell is going on?" I raised my voice. I needed answers, now!

"Quiet. Not now." Torrez placed his arm on the seat of the taxi and turned to look out the back window.

"Do you think he followed us?" Obviously, he was checking to see if Greco was behind us.

Torrez scrunched his brow and motioned toward the cabbie. "I'll tell you when we're alone."

Chapter 7

Torrez stared out the window for the duration of the one-hour taxi ride.

He kept his hands in fists and his shoulders high. He was deep in thought, and he appeared to have no plans to share them with me.

I could have jumped out and run and he wouldn't have noticed.

The taxi dropped us off at the Quincy Suites in Milton. As Torrez checked in, I walked past a vibrant flower arrangement and grand piano. The classy colonial decor reminded me I was back in Boston, and part of me was impressed he didn't pick a seedy motel.

Torrez guided me to the second floor and held his arm out, palm flat, motioning for me to stay back. He pressed his body against the wall outside room 201B. He reached under his shirt and withdrew a gun from a holster near his armpit. With his eyes scanning up and down the corridor, he swiped the keycard and kicked the door open. He crouched down, turned the lights on, and pointed the gun to each corner of the room.

And while he appeared ridiculous, protecting me from... air, he also looked sexy. His jeans bunched up around his rock hard ass and pulled tight around his thighs. With the muscles in his arms flexed and his jaw set, I could easily picture him as a badass Navy SEAL taking down a terrorist.

He straightened and lowered his gun. "Clear. Enter."

The room smelled of bleach and fresh linens. A quilted cranberry bedspread covered the double bed, and paintings of ships in a harbor adorned the walls. "Do you do that everywhere you go, or was that just to impress me?"

He placed his gun on the table near the door, barrel pointed toward the window. "Were you impressed?"

"Not really." I lied. I'd never tell him the way he handled a gun like a third arm turned me on. As soon as the door to the hotel room shut, I faced him down. "We're alone now. Tell me."

"Tell you what?" He threw his bag on the luggage stand and turned to me with his hands on his hips.

"What do you mean tell you what? Why the hell are we in a hotel room in Milton?"

"Just sit down and shut up. We're safe here for the night."

Excuse me? "Stop telling me to shut up. We weren't safe at your place?"

"No. I need to make some calls. Please just have a seat. Or take a nap or something." His open hand motioned to the end of the bed, brushing me off like a child.

I propped my fists on my hips and stepped in, forcing him to look me in the eye. "Stop trying to get rid of me! You dragged me into this mess, and now you want to pretend I'm not here?"

He sighed and looked to the ceiling. When he brought his gaze back to mine, his eyes burned with scary intensity. "I'm not pretending you're not here. Believe me. You bein' here is why I'm doing everything I'm doing. It's all for you."

"It is?" Torrez eternally contradicted himself. Ignoring me, being rude to me, but supposedly all this was for me?

"Yes. So the first thing I need to do for you is make some calls. You need to get back on Eastern time, so sleep or the jetlag will get ya."

"I've made this trip many times and I'm perfectly aware how to handle the jetlag." Moan for a week until it goes away. "I don't have anything to sleep in." I'd been wearing this skirt and blouse for a full day now. My toes felt permanently molded into the front of my heels.

He dug in his bag and offered me a solid black tee. "Here."

It smelled good when I sniffed it, but I pretended it smelled bad.

"There're probably toothbrushes in the bathroom. You can shower."

"I don't have any clean underwear."

"That is not my problem," he snapped back.

It most definitely was. He created this mess. "It wouldn't be my problem either if I had some luggage." My voice pitched up at the end. I'd had enough of him and his rudeness.

A muscle in his jaw ticked and he spoke with strained harshness. "We'll get you clothes tomorrow when the stores open."

He expected me to sleep with no underwear in the one bed in the room with him? "Can we call the lobby and see if they have any women's clothing?"

"Fine." He called the front desk and asked for clothes. He hung up. "They don't have any clothes, but they'll bring by some robes."

"Good."

Torrez paced the room, impatiently waiting for something.

A knock on the door sounded, and he turned to face it with his elbows and knees bent.

"Room service," a tiny female voice called from the other side of the door.

He gripped his gun, peered through the peephole, then moved the curtains aside to peek out the window.

"It's just the robes, Torrez. Open the door."

He cracked the door and pulled the terrycloth through. He handed me a folded robe. "Here."

"Oh thank you, kind sir."

He pulled a second phone from his coat pocket and pressed the screen.

I couldn't hear him well, but it seemed like he called someone named Dallas and then someone named Rogan. His third call, he spoke louder, but he rattled off rapid-fire Spanish to someone I inferred was named Falcon. I spoke four languages, but none of them were of Spanish origin. I understood a few words he said like *truck, yes and no, Greco, Soraya, Milton*. He kept looking at me and rubbing his hand over his face.

The calls took so long I showered, put on the robe, and fell asleep to the sounds of him speaking to Falcon in Spanish.

Hours later, he climbed into the bed beside me. I stiffened and scooted closer to my edge.

"Don't worry, princess. I won't touch you." His voice sounded gravelly and tired.

Even though his oversized body took up half the bed, he managed to keep a respectable distance between us. I tried to get as comfortable as I could with scratchy sheets and his energy bombarding me. His breathing was quiet, and he didn't say anything, but his presence screamed, *I am Torrez, and I'm right next to you, and you know you fucking want me to touch you so don't even try to pretend*. After a while, his body stopped yelling at me, and quiet blanketed the room.

I turned over slowly to check him out. God, he looked gorgeous when he slept. I'd noticed it the first night, but tonight it was more obvious. The harsh edges of his smile softened when he slept. His mouth opened slightly. The broad, flat planes of his cheeks seemed more rounded. The aggression left him, and an uncharacteristic vulnerability overtook his features.

His right eye popped open. Oops, caught me staring.

"It'll be okay. I promise." His voice rasped low through the quiet room.

"What will be okay?"

"Everything. I'll make it okay."

I nodded. He kept talking. "I gotta make a decision about the way I want my life to go from now on. A choice that's been pullin' at me for a long time."

His big hand swooped up and cupped my neck. I tightened up, but his grip grew more firm. The glint in his eyes begged me to give in. He needed comfort. And as much as I hated him, I wanted to give that to him. I let his hand pull my head to his chest. The unyielding wall of his pecs warmed my forehead.

"What kinda choice?" I asked his chest.

He took a deep breath and spoke slowly. "I've been drifting with the current. Letting the wind pressure me to do things against my values to keep the waters calm." His thumb rubbed my chin, slightly putting pressure there until I lifted my head and looked in his eyes. "But security is a false perception. By not fighting back, I've drifted deeper into the storm."

"I'm not sure exactly what you mean, but I think I get you."

"Do you?"

"About not fighting back. Letting your fears win doesn't solve the problem."

"No. It doesn't. And what are you afraid of, Soraya? Right now, what's scaring you?"

He'd shared something private with me, so I felt obligated to be honest with him. "I'm afraid to dream." I kept it vague, hoping he'd drop it.

He kissed my forehead. "Tell me."

I shook my head. No. I couldn't trust him with my deepest insecurities.

He moved down till we were eye to eye. His fingers worked into my hair and scratched my scalp. "Knowing the truth from you would help guide my decisions tonight, but you're closing down."

We weren't talking about Yegor anymore. He was asking me how I felt about him. "I'm afraid you're not real."

His fingers squeezed in my hair. "I know."

"You do?"

"Yes. You don't trust me. But you want to, right?"

"There's a part of me. Deep inside that has hope, you know? This optimistic thread that's buried under all the crap in my life. Despite my circumstances, it's like, for the first time, I have a chance. I'm out of Yegor's grasp. He doesn't even know where I am."

"Right. Is that the first time?"

"Yes. First time ever. And the possibilities are blowing my mind. I could do so much without his tyranny over my head. But then all that depends on you. And the thread inside me really wants to believe in you. But a bigger part of me is telling me I'm in deeper trouble than I ever was."

He gently pressed his lips to mine. First just the middle of our lips touched, but he moved in slowly and gave me a full kiss. I didn't pull away because it felt good. His lips conveyed affection and kindness, both of which I needed as much as he did.

"Thanks for telling me how you feel. I wish I could say you could trust me, but the truth is I don't know what's gonna happen. I know what I want to happen, but it requires me to turn my ship around and wade through some thick waters to get back on course."

I nodded because I appreciated him telling me the truth. We were deep in trouble, and he might never be the man I needed. His hand left my hair, he rolled away, and closed his eyes.

The thread of hope in my heart disintegrated. Life doesn't work out easy for me. Men never came through for me. Men disappointed and hurt me all the time. All I had was myself.

I WOKE WITH HIS BIG heater of a body behind me, my robe partially open, the warmth of his strong palm resting on my abdomen. I should've pulled away. But his embrace comforted me like a flannel blanket in a blizzard. The day hadn't broken. Darkness still coated the room, but a hint of light gray highlighted the edges of the curtains. The only noise was the air unit running near the window and the delicious hum of his breath tickling my ear in a steady, relaxed rhythm.

His chest rose and fell against my back. His hand skimmed up to just under my breasts, then back down in a gentle caress. I held my breath and my mouth went dry. His lips moved to my ear and his fingers pressed flat. I stayed still, pretending to be sleeping.

I was angry with him. I couldn't trust him. He'd hurt me before. And yet there was no way I could say no to his pleading touch.

When he tugged on the collar of my robe, I wiggled my shoulder and pulled my arm out. His hand traced from my elbow to my fingers, and trailed down my thigh. He wrapped his fingers around my knee and lifted, placing my shin on his leg and opening me up to him. Suddenly, I couldn't remember why I should fight it. I forgot the horrible things he'd said and the confusing danger we were in. All I could feel was fire burning through me. My core ached for him to touch me. There. Just put your hand there, please.

And he did. Slow and quiet. Like he was afraid to spook me, but still confident, like he had permission. Which he did not.

I was about to stop his hand moving south when his lips pressed a sensuous kiss behind my ear. With that, I was lost. I couldn't say no anymore. Torrez could have whatever he wanted.

"Need you," he rasped near my ear. His hips pressed a hard erection to my lower back. "God, need to fuck you so bad." His hand cupped my sex and I felt it. He wasn't lying. He needed me desperately.

I raised an arm and wrapped it around his head behind me. My fingers scratched through the short hair on his perfectly round scalp. The raw power of his strength surprised me again. This man could probably smash a pumpkin between two fingers. Yet, he caressed my skin like I was made of eggshells.

I was totally open for his hands to explore. The hand at my crotch massaged up and down. His other hand came around and pulled my robe fully open. He gripped my left breast. "Want you. Say I can have you."

I grunted.

"Say I can have you. Say I can bury myself inside you and forget everything. Need that right now more than I've ever needed anything in my life." He rose up on one elbow and kissed from my neck to my chin. He spoke at my lips. "Say I can kiss you."

"Yes," I whispered.

His lips brushed mine. It was an odd angle, but incredibly hot. "Tell me."

"You can kiss me."

He moved on top of me, pressing me fully to my back. He was wearing boxer briefs and nothing else. His immense frame swamped my conscience. No hotel room. No Yegor or Veranistaad. Only a man and a woman in a bed who needed each other fiercely. Maybe for different reasons, but I needed this too. After all the uncertainty of leaving and last night, he grounded me.

When he kissed me, questions floated between our lips. What does this mean? Who are you to me?

"Relax," he whispered.

And I did. I enjoyed his kiss and blocked all my negative thoughts. I'd committed to this now, no going back. His rock hard dick pressed against my sex, and I wanted nothing more than to feel it move inside me again. My hands slipped his briefs down and off, and I shivered at the raw nakedness between us. Not only our bodies, our souls were bared too.

His hands skated down my sides. "You on the pill?"

"Yes."

"I wanna take you raw like this."

God, that would be fantastic. I wrapped my legs around him and tilted my hips. His hand worked his tip at my entrance and he groaned. "Yes, please. Say I can have you like this."

"You can have me. Do it."

We both moaned as he slid inside. All kinds of receptors triggered as the hot, hard pressure filled me. God. He was beautiful.

He thrust all the way in and we were one. For a brief second I froze. Perhaps this was a mistake. He could hurt me so badly. But then he moved, and I knew I'd take any consequence he threw at me later.

I grabbed his shoulders and lavished them as they rippled. My hands explored his back and his ass. Holy crow, what a tight round ass undulating beneath my fingers. All his muscles coiled, drilling his intensity into me. I loved it.

He reached a hand down to touch my clit and I gasped. So good. He moved faster. The pleasure grew out of control. No way to hold it back. I felt it welling up and bursting from me with a blast of air. He pummeled into me full speed. My hips met his pound for pound. "God, yes," I cried out. His endless pumping extended my orgasm forever.

He sped up to a ruthless pace. God, how could he last so long? I didn't last a minute. "Good?" I asked him.

"So goddamn good. Don't want to lose it."

"No. Come. Let go. Let it all go."

His head dropped, and he sucked my breast into his mouth. He moaned around my nipple as he came with a loud grunt followed by a long moan. His whole body tensed and shook with incredible power. He expressed it so clearly, it drew another wave of pleasure through my body and dragged my own orgasm out even longer. I was riding the longest wave of my life.

His scruffy jaw scraped behind my ear as he moved slowly in and out through the slick wetness. "Thank you, babe."

The fire inside me flared up at his affectionately calling me *babe*. As if I could be his babe. As if things could be different between us.

I sighed and closed my eyes. Being with Torrez hit me hard. Feeling so emotionally connected yet watching him slip through my fingers like sand. A temporary bliss in a sea of uncertainty and pain.

This moment would pass with the rising sun. Torrez would return to being an ass and hauling me around against my will. I had to worry about myself, not whatever business deal had gone bad with him and his criminal friend.

I lay still for a moment till he pulled out. If he sensed me closing down, he didn't say anything. He rolled to his back and remained quiet. He didn't comfort me because he couldn't tell me the words I ached for or promise me anything. And I didn't want him to anyway.

Actually, maybe I was lying to myself.

If he said he loved me, I'd probably believe him. I might even say it back.

Chapter 8

Harsh grunts woke me from my sleep. Torrez sat on his ass on the floor, no shirt—holy crap, he was cut—doing sit ups. Not just doing them, crunching his body like he had a walnut in his navel and he needed to crack it open in order to survive.

He tilted his head and peeked at me with one green eye. "Mornin', sleeping beauty," he muttered between grunts.

"Uh, morning." He must've covered me with my robe after we drifted off last night because it draped loosely around my body. I snaked my arms through the sleeves and pulled the tie tight.

Oh goodness. Last night. I cowered inside preparing for bad news. Torrez would surely dump me here. I gave in and he got what he wanted. Now he'd drop me like a dead body and carry on with his secret mission without me dragging him down.

He stilled with a loud exhale and rested his elbows on his knees. He wiped a glorious shine of sweat from his brow with a hotel towel.

"You gotta wear your travel clothes for right now." He dropped back down to the carpet to resume his routine.

I just stared at him, not understanding what he said. Oh man, I could watch him do shirtless crunches and listen to his grunts forever. The tattoos on his biceps and chest shined with perspiration, his cut-off sweats revealed strong muscular legs. My stomach flipped thinking about his hot body pressed up against mine last night. The way his huge cock filled me and his hand teased my clit.

"We're going on a shopping spree." His voice pulled me out of my memories.

Did I hear him right? "We are?"

He popped up to his full height and wiped down his abs. I'd never wanted to be a hotel towel before in my life.

"Got a rental car delivered here."

He did? When I was sleeping? "Oh."

"You need to buy a bunch of clothes and anything you need. Nice stuff, casual stuff, summer weather, be prepared."

That didn't sound like I was getting kicked to the curb in Milton, Massachusetts. And a shopping spree would be exciting. Yegor always controlled my clothing and shopping. I had some freedom when I was here for school, but there was always the chance he'd come check on me.

"Why are we getting a rental car and going shopping?"

"I made a decision."

He'd mentioned a decision last night. "About which way your life should go?"

"Yes." He grinned and winked at me.

Oh God. Before we had sex, he wasn't sure and this morning he'd made his decision. No pressure. I was either horrible in bed, and he was taking me shopping to send me on my way, or he loved it and we were buying clothes and staying together. Which way did I want this to go?

"And that would be?"

"Road trip."

that was it. He hated it and was giving me the boot. "Road trip?" My voice squeaked. "Where am I going?"

"*We're* going to North Carolina. Ever been there?"

We're going? Together? And I'd need a lot of clothes? Relief washed through me and anger too. Why did my life rest on his stupid decision?

"I'm not going on any road trip with you."

He tossed his towel on the floor and took two steps toward me. "You have no choice."

"I have any choice I want."

"You don't. Okay. Let's say it was up to you. What're you gonna do?" He opened his arms wide and motioned around the room. Oy vey, his body was a work of art. Skin the color of a mocha latte, patches of tattoos across the broad planes of his pecs, and abs that even at rest, had bumps in all the right places. His shorts hung low on his hips, and my eyes fixated on the perfect groove of thick muscles pointing down in a tantalizing *V* to his groin. How many nuts did he have to crack in his belly button to get those there?

Focus, Soraya. Don't let his near nakedness distract you. "I'm gonna stay with Zook and Cecelia." I crossed my arms under my boobs and stood tall.

"Zook's in Montana and thinks you're safer with me."

Drat. That was true. "I'll go out on my own."

"Oh really? With what money?"

He knew he had me. He was toying with me. "I don't know. I can get a modeling gig."

"Modeling?" One of his dark eyebrows arched.

"Right before graduation, an agent approached me and offered me a modeling contract."

"He did?" His lips quirked up in a smarmy smile.

"Yes, but I was leaving the country so I turned him down."

"Not that you don't have what it takes to be a model, because you do. But due respect, that guy was probably a fraud."

"No he wasn't. He had a nice card. He's from a respected modeling agency. He said he could get me print work right away. And shows once I went through their intake process."

"Hmm." His thumb and forefinger rubbed the scruff that had grown on his chin overnight. I'd admired his watch on the trip home, but now seeing him wearing it while shirtless, I loved it.

The big face and thick black band made him seem important, in charge, and in control.

"What? You don't believe me?" It totally happened. I really considered calling him after graduation, but Yegor and Maksim had guards escort us back home.

"I believe you. I also believe he wanted in your pants." He perched his hands on his hips causing his biceps to pop out. Lordy, lordy.

"He didn't. He didn't even hit on me." I got a slimy vibe from the dude, but he didn't hit on me.

"And how much did he want from you to make you a model?"

God, I hated his *I'm smarter than you because I'm older and wiser* attitude. So cocky. "He didn't say."

"Ah, there's the rub. They don't do that shit for free. They ask for a few grand to make you a portfolio. Give you some catwalk classes. Next thing you know, they ghost you, and you're down a few grand."

I wasn't going to win this one, and I seriously needed some clothes. I'd let him take me shopping and then find a way to get away from him, taking my loot with me.

"Okay. I'll allow you to take me shopping."

He chuckled. "It'll be my pleasure. Where is your favorite place to shop?"

Hmm. "Nothing beats shopping in the Big Apple." I said it to test him. Shopping in New York was expensive and hectic, but also incredibly fun. Would he take me there?

"We can do that. Be there in four hours or so."

I'D NEVER ADMIT IT to him but I had a blast shopping with Torrez in Midtown, Manhattan. After he withdrew a duffle bag full of cash from the bank, we took a taxi downtown and strolled up Madison Avenue. I felt like a total tourist looking up at the towering skyscrapers, but he looked comfortable walking fast, picking and choosing luxury stores to peruse.

Anything I looked at or tried on, he gave to a clerk to wrap for me. He paid cash for everything. The clerks' eyes would bug out when he pulled hundreds from his wallet.

I picked out some cute pajamas at Kate Spade, jeans that fit like a glove and had bright stitching up the sides and on the pockets, killer Louis Vuitton heels that would make Khloé Kardashian jealous, and makeup for all seasons from Sephora.

Buying the dresses thrilled me the most. I splurged and bought risque dresses I'd always wanted to wear but never could. I held my breath when he walked into the Cartier store and strutted up to the counter without thinking twice. He pointed to a one-inch thick choker necklace with five rows of pave-set square diamonds. "You'll need this."

The price tag said twenty-five thousand dollars! The magical piece sparkled like it was plugged into floodlights. The clerk wrapped it up, and Torrez grinned as he added it to our bags.

I was so shocked I couldn't even say thank you. When in the world would I *need* a necklace like that? But hey, if it made him happy, I wasn't gonna protest.

"Let's see that one." He pointed out a thinner diamond chain with a unique agrafe clasp. The hook-and-loop fastening hung shorter around the neck, but the long tail dangled down at least a foot. "Take this off."

A lump formed in my throat as he reached behind my neck and found the clasp of my NB Oil necklace. He messed with it for a second before he grunted and tugged it off, pulling the thin hairs at the base of my neck that were stuck in it.

"Turn around." He took the new chain, delicate and pretty, and I looked down, my heart pounding as he fastened it. His hands turned me by my shoulders. He adjusted the longer part to hang between my breasts, dipping under the V of my shirt. He kissed my ear. "Gorgeous and sexy. You're free. You don't have to wear it."

Free. He gave me that. *You don't have to wear it*. He also gave me the choice. Yegor had forced me to wear my NB Oil necklace since I turned seventeen. Finally, I was free. "I'll wear it. I love it. Thank you." My voice cracked, but I didn't cry. I was too happy to cry.

He paid the Cartier clerk with a credit card, which surprised me, but I suppose he wouldn't carry that much cash around in a duffle bag. Would he?

A satisfied smile lit up his eyes, and he grasped my hand, guiding me back out to the busy street. Torrez bought a sleek Armani suit before walking me past the Empire State Building to the Manhattan Mall. There, he purchased some kickass T-shirts from a Harley Davidson store, cargo pants, boots, snow gear, and beach stuff. He made a point to pick me out a red suede cowboy hat from Macy's. By the time we had finished, I had no idea where we were going, but we were ready for it.

We stopped and had lunch at an outdoor cafe at the base of three tall skyscrapers. New Yorkers and tourists walked quickly by, cars honked, and the air smelled of burnt toast. He fit right into the scene. He ate like a monkey, but he surprised me with his lighthearted conversation and his ironic sense of humor. He paid cash again and left a life-changing tip for the waitress.

We piled all the bags in the trunk of a taxi and hit traffic waiting to enter the Lincoln Tunnel under the Hudson River. As the taxi entered the dark tunnel and the echo of engines filled the cab, I tensed. I'd been in tunnels before but never one under the water and never one over a mile long. He took my hand and ran a thumb over the back of my palm.

Once we were back in the rental car and on the highway, I decided to ask the question I'd asked him several times today, but he refused to reply. "So why are we going to North Carolina again?"

"Gotta meet a guy named Falcon."

Oh. He answered me. Maybe he needed the privacy of the car before he could speak freely about his plans.

"Is that the guy you were speaking Spanish to last night?"

"Yep. He's gonna style us out."

"With what?"

"Getting us where we're going."

"I thought we were going to North Carolina."

"I mean where we're going after we leave Falcon's place."

After? "We're not going back to Boston?"

"No. I told you. Road trip."

Shoot. I'd gotten so wrapped up in shopping I'd forgotten my plan to get my stash and run. Selling the diamond choker would give me some money to get away from Torrez and get started somewhere, then I'd get a job and never see him again. "I'm not going on any road trip with you," I stated firmly.

"Too late. We're already on the road." He nodded at the front windshield.

"Let me out now."

"Nope." He kept his eyes on the car in front of him, but I nailed him with my glare.

"I'll run." I meant it too. I'd run off with all my stuff. Now it would be hard to run through this tunnel carrying all those bags, but in theory, I would run.

"You won't get far."

Darn. He was probably right. "Are you kidnapping me?"

"Me? No." He drew out the *O* of *No*.

"You're kidnapping me. What the hell?"

"Relax, princess. It'll be fun."

"Fun? Kidnapped and forced on a road trip sounds fun to you?"

"Yes. If you're with me, it does."

"What do you know about fun?" Torrez Lavonte and fun didn't seem to go together, despite him entertaining me today on our shopping spree.

"I'm fun," he said, unconvincingly.

"Sure you are."

"I am."

"You're the opposite of fun. You're a serious soldier dude."

"Sailor." He sounded annoyed. "Navy."

"Whatever."

"Not whatever. Don't mix those up." Yes, definitely annoyed by that one.

"Fine. You seem like a hardcore Navy dude. You probably spend your weekends preparing for armageddon."

His eyes pulled from the road and cut to mine. "Is that what you think we do?

"And when you're done you eat nails and kill puppies."

"It's not like that. Besides, I've been retired ten years. Make my own fun now."

"Like what?"

"You wanna know what I do for fun?"

"Yes."

"Hold on." He tapped on his phone. "Falcon, Soraya wants to know what I do for fun. Where's BRX hot right now?" He looked at me. "He's checking." He listened again. "Sweet. We're taking a detour. We'll be in Wilmington tomorrow night." He listened some more and his brow furrowed. "It's a date. You're not invited."

A date? And this Falcon person wanted to come? Torrez broke out into his rapid-fire Spanish. His shoulders tensed and he clenched his jaw.

After several grunts, he switched back to English. "Fine. We'll meet you at PNC at 1800 tomorrow." He tossed his phone into the console between us. "Falcon's meeting us in Raleigh, North Carolina. BRX semi-finals going on tomorrow night."

Okay. There was a lot there I needed to ask him about, but I decided to start with BRX.

"What's BRX?"

"Bull Riders Extreme."

Now if he'd said it was a shooting range or a nightclub, I wouldn't have been surprised, but bulls? "Bulls?"

"Yes."

"Your fun involves a bull? Like with horns?"

"Yep."

"Holy cow."

"No fun riding a cow."

"You ride the bulls?"

"I have ridden many bulls. Tonight we'll be spectators. It's fun to watch. No one will even know we're there."

He'd ridden many bulls and was a Navy SEAL? He didn't mess around. "How did you end up riding bulls?"

"My dad was a professional bull rider. Before BRX, we traveled the rodeo circuit with him. He was one of the founders of BRX about twenty years ago. Huge events with just bulls. No horse events, no roping cows. Just man versus bull."

I'd seen commercials for bull riding events, but always passed over it because it looked terrifying. "I've heard of BRX. It's on TV, right?"

"Yeah, it's taken off bigger than he ever expected. I guess people enjoy watching a man get whipped off a bull with a high potential of being stomped to death." He smiled to himself.

"Where did your dad learn to ride a bull?"

"Brazil." He said the *Z* like an *S*.

"You're Brazilian?"

"I was born in Texas, but yes, half Brazilian." I never would have guessed Brazilian.

"What's the other half?"

"Full-bred mutt. My mom was French, Puerto Rican, and a sprinkling of random shit her grandma threw in there."

"I see." Whatever ethnicities came together to form Torrez, it was the perfect mix. The man was shockingly stunning. "Do you speak... What language do they speak in Brazil?"

"Mostly Portuguese. My dad spoke Portuguese to me, so I learned it from him. Picked up Tex Mex and a bunch of Mexican slang on the road."

"So you speak full-bred mutt too?"

"Basically."

"You're a very interesting person."

"Thank you. So are you." The sweet smile he gave me forced me to look away. I couldn't handle him being sweet. We were enemies after all.

As the city limits faded behind us and the highway became lined with trees, I sat back in my chair and tried to relax. "Tell me more about your dad." I mean if we had at least a ten-hour car ride ahead of us, we might as well chat.

"He came out to the States to ride the circuit and met my mom in Alabama. She rode the barrels and loved trick riding. She was insane. Hanging by one foot from a stirrup with a horse at full gallop. My dad fell hard for her. A daredevil like himself. We lived like nomads, following bulls around the country. My given name is Tourino Bravo Durango Lavonte. Touro Bravo means fighting bull. My parents called me Tor. My Navy buddies gave me the nickname Torrez the Bull with a *Z* instead of an *S*."

Torrez shared with me easily. Like he trusted me. I liked his openness. "Does Torrez mean bull?"

"No, but the guys didn't know that. I told them and they liked it more because it bothered me. It stuck and here I am, Torrez Lavonte."

Here he was in all his greatness. And his assholeness. "Did you want to be a bull rider like your dad?"

He nodded. "When I was a kid, I thought I'd be a world champ like my dad."

"World champion?"

"Yeah. Three times. He had natural talent for it, but he sacrificed everything to make it to the top."

"Wow." So his father lived large and brave like he did.

"He put a lot of pressure on me to live up to the Lavonte legacy. Everywhere I went, riders would say they couldn't wait to see what I'd do on the bull. But there's a lot more failures than successes in bull riding. More often than not injuries end careers, if not lives."

The thought of a young Torrez getting stomped to death did not sit well with me. "So you didn't ride?"

"Oh, I did. He had me riding sheep since I was a toddler. Rode a calf before I rode a bike. I did junior rodeo through grade school and high school. Placed pretty well. Broke my arm, busted my ribs. Came back to win a BRX regional championship my first year on the pro circuit."

"You must've been amazing."

"A few people thought so. Not my dad. He'd come up to me after every ride and say it coulda been better. Said the judges were favoring me because I was his kid. Not once did he give me a compliment or even a *good job*."

He won a championship and his dad never said good job? "So what happened?"

"I realized I'd never please him, and bull riding wasn't what I really wanted to do."

"What did you really want to do?"

"Jump out of planes. I joined the Navy."

I laughed. "You went from one dangerous profession to another."

"Nah. You faced a bull, you faced a terrorist. Same thing."

"Except bulls don't have guns and bombs."

"Nope. Horns and hooves and two thousand pounds of pissed-off animal."

So he wasn't close with his dad. "Where's your dad now?"

"Dead. Lived by the bull, died by the bull."

"A bull killed him?"

"Yes. His hand got stuck in the flank strap. Bull stomped his legs. Landed one to his skull. I was twenty-nine. He was way too old to get on that bull." He shook his head. "How about you? Where are your parents?" he asked, clearly done opening up and wanting to change the subject.

"Uh, I don't know." My fingers traced the swirling pattern of the red stitching on my jeans.

"You don't know?"

Did I want to tell him this? I'd never told anyone. "Ivan and his former wife, Nadya, adopted me as a baby. They raised me until I was old enough to go to boarding school."

"That sounds very distant. Yegor was his son?"

"Yes."

"So was he your brother?"

See, there was no easy way to explain the madness that had been my life. "No. They told me he would be my husband."

"That's odd."

That was an understatement. "Luckily, I don't remember my childhood."

He raised one eyebrow at me. "It's just blank?"

"Yeah. My first memories are when I was sixteen. Sometimes I think I remember things, but they're so impossible, I know they must be dreams."

"What kinds of things?"

"T.V. shows. Children's books. Goodnight Moon. Curious George. They all feel familiar when I see them, but I know there's no way I would've seen those things in Veranistaad. When I went to the States to attend Hale, it was surreal. Felt like home. I wanted to stay there."

"Why didn't you?"

"Stay? I'd have to fight Yegor. I couldn't do that on my own. I thought I needed someone to rescue me. I got myself a boyfriend. It didn't work out with him."

"Why?"

"He'd get angry. Hit me."

"Hit you?" His eyes cut to mine and his voice got deep.

"Yes. A few times."

A muscle in his neck flexed, and his knuckles turned white from gripping the wheel. Uh oh. I'd angered the bull. "You went back after the first time?"

"I did. I was desperate. I wanted to stay so bad. But I finally realized he wasn't going to fight Yegor for me, so I gave up and went back to Veranistaad. When you showed up, I thought you were there to rescue me."

"And you decided we should fuck?"

"No. I decided to fantasize about it. I thought it would be... romantic. If we were lovers and escaped together. Until I found out you were such a turkey."

"Hey."

"You earned it."

"But I made up for it this morning. Didn't I?"

Heat burned my cheeks. "That didn't make up for anything. You still have a lot of groveling to do."

"Is that so?"

I nodded.

"You mean if I reached between your legs right now, here on the highway, you'd push me away?"

"Yes."

"Open your legs."

"No."

He reached over the console and placed his hand on my thigh. The warmth of his fingers sank quickly through my jeans. "Let Torrez work some magic down there." He didn't move his hand, and it wasn't anywhere near my private parts, but the touch felt extremely intimate. It would actually be hot to let him touch me while we drove, but Mr. Lavonte was getting a big head after getting away with what he did last night, and he needed a reality check.

"Ain't happening." I lifted his hand off my thigh.

He clicked his tongue and shook his head. "Aye, que linda e teimosa."

"Who's Linda?"

"You. Means beautiful in Portuguese."

Well, that was nice. "What does teimosa mean?"

"Means stubborn." He winked and quirked his lip like this was a compliment.

Excuse me? "I'm not teimosa."

"You define teimosa."

"Whatever." Wasn't going to fight with him anymore.

"It's okay, Teimosa. Promise you by the end of this trip, you'll be begging for my hand between your legs."

Oh my god, the man was impossible! "Don't get your hopes up, Tauro Bravo."

He laughed. "We'll stop in Baltimore for sleep. Finish the last leg to Raleigh tomorrow."

Uh oh. Another hotel?

"I'd like my own bed." I had to take a stand or last night would repeat.

His eyes narrowed. "You want your own bed?" He sounded shocked and offended. Yes, he'd been generous with me today, but money meant nothing when it came to matters of the heart. Yegor had money and he used it to control me.

I'd enjoyed 'Torrez' company today, and BRX did sound fun, but the fact remained, he'd hurt me, he'd forced me to go on this trip, and he couldn't be trusted.

"That's what I said."

"Alright." He frowned and turned his gaze back to the road.

Chapter 9

Torrez

I respected her wishes last night. Slept in a second bed in the room. I'd give her that if she needed it. But tonight, the woman made herself even more drop-dead gorgeous, and I couldn't promise keeping my distance much longer.

Soraya fidgeted with the tassel on her red hat as she held it on her lap. Her new jeans had thick red stitching up the sides and fit her like she'd poured them on those hips. She poofed up her hair and went all out with makeup, matching boots, a thick belt, and lots of silver jewelry. She didn't wear the choker, but kept the thinner chain I'd bought her. We parked at the southern end of the PNC lot, away from the crowds and other cars. "We're here."

She arched her neck to look around, then back at me as she plopped the hat on her head, flattening her pretty brown hair to her forehead, and offering me an excited smile. Looking at her like that, letting her beauty smack me in the face, I saw something so pure and true, I had to tell her. "You were never meant to be a Russian princess."

Her eyes widened before she looked down to hide a sad blush. She'd probably never talked about it before. Shit, she didn't even talk to me about it before we fucked the first time, but Soraya needed to hear her truth now.

"You were hiding under that crown. This is who you're meant to be. Big hair, wide smile, so colorful and bright you blind a man."

Her stunned face shifted into a grin that grew from deep in her heart. Anybody could tell her she was pretty. Probably many men had, but I bet no one had taken the time to really get to know her. "And I'll tell you there's nothing more attractive to a man than a woman being her true self. You found it, babe. Don't let it go. It's captivating. It's rare. And I'm lucky to be here to see it."

Her mouth dropped open and she whispered, "Thank you."

"Let's go. You're gonna love this." I grabbed her hand and left the car where the rental agency would pick it up. We were getting a new ride from Falcon tonight.

The BRX crowd filled the lot with cowboys, barbeques, and rodeo bunnies. I wore dark jeans, a brown suede button-down shirt, and a felt hat with a bull-rider's crease. We'd blend in without being noticed, no problem.

At the east side of the lot, parked beyond the main tailgate area, I spotted a huge RV with black racing stripes against a faux wood texture. Standing next to it, Falcon. Six-foot-seven, pushing two hundred pounds, back against the door, arms and legs crossed, long hair tied at his neck, dark shades and a sloppy Satanic goatee.

Soraya's hand tightened in mine as we approached him. "Falcon. Soraya." Her shoulders relaxed when I wrapped an arm around her, placing enough pressure on her bicep to say *you're safe with me*. My hand there also sent a clear message to Falcon. *Mine*.

He tipped his head. She gave him a tense smile, clearly baffled why we were meeting this shady character at a BRX show.

The answer was Dallas Monroe referred me to Rogan Saxton, who sent Falcon. I met Rogan and Falcon after the standoff at Dallas's wedding six years ago. Falcon provided backup as Rogan faced down the capo of the Dubare Syndicate in the alley behind the church. Rogan handled that nightmare with style. Two women in the car and he held his fire till the exact moment for maximum effectiveness. Rogan claimed Falcon was Delta and solid. He'd have to be to make Special Ops. But unless we spent time in combat together, which we had not, he was unproven to me and would need to earn my trust.

I tossed him the keys to the rental car. "South end of the lot. Blue Tahoe. License 9ZXH849. Get all our shit and put it in the new vehicle."

He caught them and stared at me without blinking.

"You did bring us a new vehicle, right?"

Falcon shook his head like he was blowing off his anger. "Yes, I brought you a vehicle."

If he couldn't follow orders, I didn't want him on my team. "Then load our shit in it and meet us at the seats."

"Yes, sir." He gave me a smarmy salute and walked to the south end of the lot. Rogan better not have sent me an insolent asshole to deal with. I had enough problems.

Keeping my hands on Soraya's waist as we climbed the stairs in the bleachers, the blaring music sent my adrenaline surging. The familiar buzz that someone could get killed or seriously injured was ironically comforting. We found our seats and sat down, leaving Falcon's open on the other side of Soraya. The announcer's booming voice introduced a rider. The gate opened. Soraya's hand flew to her mouth when the hopeful cowboy hit the dirt.

Falcon joined us as the next bull rider burst out of the shoot. He flailed in the air as the bull bucked, but this hot-shot rookie was trying to prove himself. He wasn't letting go for shit, and that bull turned on him at least four times. Sometimes sheer determination can be the deciding factor.

The rider and the bull put on a great show, bringing everyone in the arena to their feet. The buzzer sounded, and the rider finally bucked off. He rolled out from under the descending hoof just in time. The bull fighters did an excellent job distracting the bull. He ran a victory lap as the lights and music pulsed like a rock concert. Soraya bounced on her toes and screamed along with the audience.

Her face glowed as she smiled at me. "This is so awesome. Those bulls are fierce."

I wrapped an arm around her shoulder and pulled her ear close to my mouth. "See. Told ya I knew how to have fun."

The music and lights cut out. The arena quieted into a hushed darkness. Falcon and I covered our weapons as a spotlight searched the crowd. "Ladies and gentlemen! It's an honor to have a celebrity among us tonight." Oh shit. Oh hell no. Please don't. "In the stands right now is none other than the great Tauro Bravo Durango Lavonte! Stand up, brother. Show us your face." Fucking shit.

The spotlight blinded me. I stepped away from Soraya. Probably too late to get her out of view, but I had to try. Falcon switched places with her and blocked her from view. I waved into the light. The audience went nuts and I smiled. Phone cameras flashed. Even if Greco's men hadn't tracked us here, my location would be revealed in seconds as everyone rushed to post the celebrity sighting. Why don't you paint a fucking bull's eye on my chest?

I gave Falcon a get-her-the-fuck-out-of-here nod. He ducked and tugged on Soraya's arm. Her bewildered face disappeared into the shadows.

The idiot in the booth continued. "Not only was Tor rookie of the year and a former East Coast champion, he's also the son of the legendary three-time world champion bull rider and founder of the BRX, the late, great Adriano Durango Lavonte."

I waved one last time as they gave props to my dad.

"We got a rank bull waiting here, Tor. You wanna suit up and climb over the rails for eight seconds of glory?"

Hell no. I tipped my hat and begged off with a laugh as I sat down. Move on, fucker.

Finally, the announcer piped down and the lights came back up. As he rambled on about tonight's champions and their scores, I slipped out of the aisle and down the stairs to the exit.

A text came through on my burner phone.

Falcon: 2 clicks west

My heart was already pounding before I took off running. Had to get back to her. Even though Falcon could handle this, having her out of my sight made my gut twist. If anything happened to her on my watch, I'd never forgive myself.

At the edge of the lot, a truck provided some cover as I scanned the circular road surrounding the venue. Nothing. After a few seconds, the huge brown RV I'd seen earlier pulled up. Falcon popped the door open and grinned at me.

I climbed in to see a frightened Soraya tied to the co-pilot's chair. Falcon had used hitch knots between her boobs to separate them and bound her hands to her thighs. "Was this necessary?" He went to town with the rope on my girl.

He glanced at her then smiled at the windshield. "Totally unnecessary."

"You fucker."

Not sure why but seeing Soraya tied up brought back a memory. Falcon with my girl. Acting like an ass.

"Did I see you at Siege before?"

"Might've." He peered into the giant side mirror and pulled out into traffic.

Yep. I definitely ran into this guy at Siege. I knew him already from the shoot out at Dallas's wedding. His hair was shorter. I was talking to a girl in a VIP booth, considering fucking her in a private room behind the glass wall, and Falcon approached with another girl. He told my girl it was time to go and she popped up, eager and excited. I was about to protest when Falcon invited me to go with them.

"You offered to share two women with me at Siege." We picked up speed as the bus headed out onto the main road leading to the highway.

"I did? Huh. Did you say yes?" He looked up at me and squinted. He couldn't remember if we'd fucked two girls together or not?

"No." I don't share shit with other men.

He nodded and kept driving, chewing on his lip. While Falcon ransacked his memory, most likely trying to remember who he fucked that night, I checked out the interior of the RV. Black suede cushions, a full kitchen, a bedroom in the back.

"What the hell is this?" I swept my hand in a grand gesture, pointing at the atrocity Falcon had brought me.

"You requested a vehicle you could sleep in." He shrugged and played stupid.

"Yeah, like a camper shell on a truck. Not a fucking tour bus."

"You gave me one day." He threw me the evil eye over his shoulder.

"I said inconspicuous."

"An RV won't raise any flags."

"Shit, man. This is overkill." It had a full-sized seating area, a decent bedroom, and shiny appliances in the kitchen.

"What you asked for wouldn't fit in anything smaller. I added a bunch of extra gear for unforeseen risks. You'll thank me later."

I never would've pegged Falcon as a geardo, but then again, he was a sniper and most snipers loved their gear and hoarded it like gold. "What's it got?"

"Can someone untie me please?" Soraya pulled my attention back to her. She grunted and struggled against the ropes. As hot as she looked tied up, Falcon crossed a line and pissed me off.

"Did you fight when he tied you up?" I spoke low to her so Falcon couldn't hear over the engine. The ropes were natural fiber and came loose easy. At least he'd done a good job.

"No. Look at him. He's huge and scary. I didn't think to fight him."

I rubbed her arms where the ropes had wrinkled her blouse. "We'll work on that."

"You wanna hear about the rig or not?" Falcon interrupted us.

I turned back to him. "Fine. Tell me."

Falcon glanced at Soraya. "Dos cargado..."

"No more Spanish. Speak in English!" Soraya said.

He paused and turned his gaze on Soraya. She flinched but persisted. "English. Slowly. So I can understand."

I ran my palm over my head and scratched behind my ear. "We're in a hurry, Teimosa."

Falcon chuckled. "You call her Teimosa?"

"Fits her. Stubborn in Portuguese."

He laughed. "Teimosa means scary in Spanish."

Oh shit. I didn't think of that. Well, it didn't matter. I'd already given it to her and the word meant stubborn to me.

Falcon was enjoying his laugh when Soraya brought us back to the conversation. "If we're in a hurry, why are we cracking jokes? It doesn't take longer to talk in English than Spanish, so speak English."

I shook my head. "There are details it's best we keep from you. And there's no time to argue about it." My voice tightened as I forced patience.

"No!" She threw her hands up. "No. Don't keep details from me. He tied me up, and now we're zooming down the interstate in an RV? Speak English or I will scream and kick and slow you down even more."

She was kinda cute trying to command two men who had her life in their hands. Regardless, I nodded at Falcon to continue, who was now all-out smiling at her. "Two MK-16s in the kitchen seats. Loaded and cleaned. Unregistered. Unmarked. I assume you have your personal carry weapons?"

"Yes."

"Multi-caliber cartridges in the cabinet next to the table." Falcon pointed a thumb over his shoulder. "Three full body armor kits in the bedroom closet."

"Why would we need body armor?" Soraya's voice hitched up.

"Intelligence center and first aid in the galley." Falcon ignored her and stuck to business. "And a shitload of gear in the basement."

"That should do it. We need more, we can stop. Anyone following?"

He checked the mirror. "Looks clear."

"Good, because no way we could outrun anyone in this tank."

"You don't like it, get your own rig. If you're going on the run, might as well do it in style."

"On the run? We're going on the run?"

I held out my hand for Soraya. "Come sit with me."

She stood slowly, and I helped her into a seat beside me at the small kitchen table. She looked at me expectantly, most likely unaware she was sitting above two fully loaded automatic weapons, even though Falcon had just stated the fact.

"We're on the run."

"We? Meaning you, me, and Falcon?"

"Not Falcon."

"Hey," he called from the driver's seat. "I'm on the run too."

"You are not," I answered back.

"I'm here. We're doing eighty-five miles per hour. I'm on the run too."

"Are we running from Greco?" Soraya asked.

"Yep. And his men."

"How many men?"

"Depends on how big he's going to make this. My guess, pretty big."

"What'd you do?"

Shit. The more she knew, the more she was at risk.

"Greco and I have a long history."

"The kind of history where he might start a fire in your apartment?"

"Yes. If he gets grumpy."

Her brow scrunched up and she pursed her lips. "When I get grumpy, I eat a Boston cream pie. I don't burn someone's place down."

"Well, he does."

"Why? Why do you allow him to do this?"

I shrugged. Excellent question. Why had I allowed Greco to pull all the strings in my life? "The money's good."

"He pays you to burn your house down?"

The irony of the way she phrased it made me chuckle. "In some ways, yes. It severely cuts into my profits if it burns down, but after I rebuild, he buys it from me."

"How bizarre."

"There's more to it than that, but it is unusual any way you look at it."

"Tell me more."

"Not right now."

"When? Because according to you, I've been kidnapped, and I'm on the run from a man who I know nothing about."

"You have not been kidnapped."

"Can I leave if I want?"

"No."

"I want to leave."

"You can't do that."

"Why not?"

"Greco saw us together. He thinks you're mine. You have to stick with me to stay safe."

Her eyes narrowed and she pinned me with her stare. "You're turning me back into a slave."

Ouch. This girl's sharp tongue cut deep. "The last few weeks, I risked losing millions of dollars I made on the palace not to mention hanging out in the armpits of Veranistaad sorting out a plan to free your ass." Her gorgeous face stiffened into an adorable scowl. Our gazes locked in a heated standoff. "I understand you're not happy with this situation and you're here against your will, but don't accuse me of making you a slave again. Have some respect."

As her bottom lip quivered and her chin scrunched up, my resolve crumbled and guilt covered me just as sure as a glossy sheen coated her big brown eyes. Okay, this was a face I never wanted to see her wear. I wrapped an arm around her shoulders and felt her go limp with a sob. "Besides you're on the run too. I shot a guard when Zook got Cecelia out. Not sure if he ID'd me or not. Did Yegor mention me or Zook?"

"He asked about you a few times. I told him I knew nothing, but yes, he could suspect you simply because you were American and from Boston where we went to school."

"Exactly. Best if you're with me for a while." She heaved another wave of tears. I pulled her to me and pressed my lips to her ear. "Hush, now."

"I'm scared."

"I know."

"And confused."

"I'm sorry."

"And tired."

"The jetlag is still messing with you. Get some sleep. When you wake up, the skies will be clearer." She swiped at her cheeks. "Look on the bright side. Ever been on a road trip in America?"

"No." The hope I'd first seen in her eyes flickered there again. She wanted so badly to believe in me, but I hadn't given her any reason to yet.

"I've traveled all over the world. Never seen anything as spectacular as this country. I'll show you places so impressive you'll forget the fact you're on the run." She nodded and her shoulders lifted. I knew she'd love an adventure. "The danger will be invisible to you. I'll shield you from it. We'll have fun. I'm fun, remember?"

"Oh god, are you gonna make me ride a bull?" She sniffled and wiped her eyes.

That drew a chuckle from deep in my gut. "You're never getting anywhere near one of those bulls." I kissed her, not sure if that was what she needed, but I had to give her something to show I cared about her. At first she didn't respond, and my lips were still curled in a smile. She finally offered me a tender kiss. The warmth of her full lips caressing mine quickly became sensual. Suddenly I wanted to give her much more than a kiss to show her how much I cared. But she was in no state for sex, and I needed to plan my next move. "Now go lie down. Try not to worry. I need to talk to Falcon."

"Okay." She stood, and I walked her to the small bed in the back. She climbed in and curled up with her head on the pillow and her legs tucked in. The urge to crawl in behind her hit me hard, but I held onto the doorway to keep me in my spot. My precious Teimosa. Maybe I should let her go. Hide her from Greco and Yegor until I kill them then set her free. She could go on with her life, have a career, be anyone she wanted to be. Maybe she'd meet a stock broker or an engineer. Someone boring who'd set her up in a house and give her babies. Darn that stung. My Teimosa making a family with someone who was not me.

Would she choose that path? Of course she would. Any woman would take security over life on the run with a criminal.

I tapped gently on the wall and headed back up to the cockpit. Falcon was still smiling.

"It's not a joke, Falcon." I kicked the ropes he'd used to tie her up with a little extra force, letting him know I did *not* appreciate his humor.

"It's funny. Running from a white-collar mafioso is child's play compared to the shit I've done."

Truth. We'd all been in much worse situations with no food, water, or transport. "Greco is no joke. He's smart and he plays dirty. If I wanted to turn, I could get him nailed for at least five murders by his own weapons, plus another ten he's ordered for the Dubare Syndicate."

"Dubare's dead. We both watched Rogan take him out a few years back."

Ah, so he remembered meeting me there. "Greco took over when Dubare died. They changed their focus to buying and selling properties, but that's all still a front for the drugs, guns, and prostitution racket."

"You tell her any of this?" He tilted his head to the back of the rig.

I took a seat and noted he'd chosen a smaller two-lane highway. We were going through a rural area. "Of course not. If she gets captured, she has to be totally clueless. I don't want them to have any reason to try to get information out of her."

"She won't get captured." He shook his head.

"Your lips to God's ears."

"It's not about praying. It's about being smart and knowing how to avoid trouble or get out quick."

"That why you want to go with me? You want to avoid trouble and get out quick?"

"Man, I'm looking for trouble."

"Rogan and Dallas aren't keeping you busy?"

"They're throwing plenty of work my way. Uneventful hostage rescues. Great pay. No action."

"Don't hope for action, Falcon."

He shrugged.

"You got a death wish?"

"Maybe."

"Great. I'm on the run from two crazy bastards and my second-in-command has a death wish."

"I'm not your second-in-command." He narrowed his eyes at me.

"You're not in command of this mission. I am." Fucker.

"I provided the vehicle, all the ammo, all the gear. I'm driving the damn bus. Rogan sent me here to help you. I'm in command."

What an arrogant prick to hijack my mission and claim command. If this were a SEAL team op, an attitude like that would get him kicked out of the plane with no parachute. "No. This is my mission. I rescued Soraya, and I'm responsible for her safety. You were supposed to drop off the transport and disappear. We had to run so you're here. That's it. You're leaving ASAP."

"What do you mean two bastards?" he asked.

"Hmm?"

"You said you're running from two crazy bastards."

"Yeah. Greco and Soraya's husband."

"She's married? Oh, this is getting good." He sat back in his chair as we passed a small town named Falcon. He pointed at the sign and chuckled.

"She is married, but against her will. A Veranistaad prince. He kept her as property. She didn't love him. He abused the hell out of her and messed with her head bad."

As I spoke, he pulled his gaze from the road and assessed me. "And you did the extraction alone?" I heard a hint of respect in his tone. Finally.

"Yeah. Had her come to the embassy. Made up a ruse about her diploma. She went to Hale."

He did a double take as he looked from the road to me again. "She's married to a prince and went to Hale?"

"Yep." Wouldn't believe it myself if it weren't absolutely true.

"What's she doing with a son of a motherless goat like you?" he asked.

"Fuck off. And I don't know. Not sure she's even with me at this point. When she finds out more, given the choice, I don't think she'd choose me. I pulled some shitty moves before I got her out. Working on earning her forgiveness."

He chewed his lip as he pondered what I'd said. "If she doesn't forgive you, can I fuck her?"

Falcon knew all the things to say to piss me right the fuck off. "No fucking Soraya."

"What if she does forgive you? Let's both fuck her."

I shook my head. "Not sharing her."

"But it would be so much fun."

I pointed an angry finger at him. "I don't wanna see your dick in any of her orifices, hear me?"

"Yes, sir." He gave me another snarky salute. Insubordinate ass.

"Clowndick."

"You shoulda been a blowjob, Torrez."

"I like you, Falc. I'm gonna fuck your sister."

He laughed. "I ain't got a sister."

"Too bad. I'll have to fuck your momma."

"Don't go there."

"Oh, poor baby can't take no one fucking his mama? Bet she gives great head. Considering you *were* a blowjob."

"Go check on your Teimosa." He raised his voice like a girl and mocked my nickname for Soraya. When I didn't laugh, he sobered up. "We'll do twelve hour shifts." There he went again, acting like he was in charge.

I pulled up a map on the on-board computer in the console. We had a choice up ahead. We could get to Atlanta via Nashville or Jackson.

"Deal. We'll stop in Jackson, Mississippi."

"What's in Mississippi?" he asked.

"Lots of bigass RVs."

"We'll fit right in."

"Yes, and you can catch a flight back to North Carolina."

"You'll see. By the time we get to Jackson, you'll be lovin' on me, wanting me to stay on."

I doubted that. "We done? I got some shit to do."

"We're done. You're on in twelve hours."

He'd drive through the night, and I'd be on in the morning. I could catch some shuteye with Soraya. Okay, maybe Falcon wasn't so bad.

Before heading back to the intelligence center Falcon had set up, I asked him, "What's the password for your intel setup?"

"Delta-bravo-nine-nine-asterisk-pound-sign-charlie-zero-oscar-eight-five-four-six—"

"Shut the fuck up."

"Okay. It's sit-on-my-face-sixty-nine."

I muttered under my breath and walked over to the laptop. Yep. His stupid password worked. I logged onto the dark web using an old handle that could never be traced to me. I ordered the first hit of my life. Prince Yegor Sharshinbaev. Doubt any sane hitman out there would pick it up since he was a foreign dignitary, but the million dollar payout might make it worth it. I'd be using the money Maksim paid me to pay the man who killed his brother.

My second job was a kill-on-sight for Luigi Greco. There'd been many hits on him over the years and no one had the balls to do it, fearing retribution from the Dubare Syndicate. I made that one five million. Someone had to take it. If they didn't, I'd kill him myself.

Third task, check for a hit on me. Nothing. Yet.

Chapter 10

Soraya

My teeth were furry. Very furry. Needed a toothbrush bad.

Last night I dreamt Torrez held me in his arms and he loved me. Without a doubt, he unconditionally worshipped me, and with him, I was safe.

A quick look around the miniature bedroom of the RV reminded me safety remained far out of reach. While I trusted Torrez had the skills to stay one step ahead of Yegor, this Greco person seemed ruthless and dangerous. Torrez hadn't told me the details, but I got the impression the stand he was taking against Greco—or in this case, the run he was making from Greco—was monumental. An epic battle at the end of a long hard war.

I peeked through the cracked bedroom door and spied the bathroom a few steps away. I could sneak out in my pajamas, brush my teeth, and slip back in without the men noticing me.

Even if they did, who cared? These red silk PJs covered my private parts, and they were pretty cute. A hot pink ribbon edged the collar and the sleeves. On the chest pocket, a set of oversized embroidered magenta lips puckered in a kiss. The white writing underneath the lips said "Swak!"

Someone had thoughtfully placed my new toiletries bag on a shelf by the door. I grabbed it and tiptoed to the bathroom. I froze when I caught sight of Falcon sitting at the table opposite the bathroom door. Luckily, he didn't hear me or see me. He sat with his shoulders hunched, head down, and a distant melancholy emanating from him.

What happened to Falcon while I'd slept? Last time I saw him, he was carefree and joking with Torrez. Now he looked like someone had burned his puppy at the stake.

I brushed that off and whooshed into the bathroom to do my business.

Hmm. Should I go bouffant and painted or natural and sunny? How does a girl do her hair and makeup when she's on the run from her abusive husband and a shady businessman? I decided to keep the makeup light and the poof in my hair at the crown of my head medium height.

When I went dark and maximum with the hair and makeup, it always attracted attention. Yegor hated even the slightest tease of my hair when I wasn't on display.

Too bad I ended up with Cage because Hale could've been the time of my life. If I had met Torrez at Siege the night Cecelia met Zook, my future could've been different. I wouldn't be on a strange bus headed for god knows where. Or maybe I would. Did Torrez run from Greco because of me? That was absurd. We'd shared two incredibly hot nights together, but this whole road trip couldn't be for me. Could it?

I opened the door with my head deep in thought, so I didn't see Falcon standing next to the kitchen table.

"Cows on my side." He spoke slowly and reflectively as he stared through the window blinds over the small dining area.

"I'm sorry?"

"Cows on my side." Wild strands of curly hair stuck out of his twisted ponytail. His dark goatee made his chiseled jaw and cheeks seem dangerous. As his sterling blue gaze pierced mine, a trickle of fear crawled up my arm like someone had released a jar of spiders in my hand.

I glanced at the bedroom door. I could scoot through quickly and pretend like I was never here. I took one slow step. When my hand hit the little handle to the door, Falcon screamed, "Cows on your side!" and pointed to the window next to me.

I jumped and my back hit the wall. "What the hell?"

"Two points for me. Zero for you," he said, unexplainably.

"Are you on drugs?" What the hell was wrong with this man?

"Didn't you see them? The cows? There were cows on my side then cows on your side. I called both sets. Two points." He talked matter of factly as he pointed to each window. I fully believed he thought he was saying something that made sense.

"Why are we calling cows?" The pungent scent of alcohol hit my nose. On the small stove in the kitchen, I spotted a glass tumbler half-full of dark liquid and an empty bottle of whiskey.

"Because it's fun. Try it. Look out the window and when you see a cow say *cows on my side*."

I looked down at my hand, which was now gripping the tiny bedroom doorknob like it could be a weapon if I pulled it loose. "I was about to get dressed."

"No." He dragged out the word and moved his head in an exaggerated circle. Oh yeah, he'd been drinking and was feeling toasty. "Those jammies are da bomb." He pointed his two fingers at my nipples tenting the fabric like he was shooting two guns at once.

"Uh." I covered my breasts with my hands.

He grinned like a kid who'd caught a peek at a nudie girl behind a curtain. "You wear those all day. No clothes."

"What?"

"Cows on my side!" He raced back to his window. "Three-zip. Catch up, Teimosa."

After a brief pause, the absurdity of it all burst from my gut in a belly laugh. How did I end up racing across the country with a crazy drunk guy and his equally nutso friend? I spent the last week crying in isolation and now I found myself here? However it happened, all I could do is what I always did. Enjoy it while it lasted.

I squinted and peeked through the blinds. "I don't see anything." The sun glinted off tall buildings in a busy city center. "There's no way you saw all those cows."

"Come closer. Look." He stepped back and motioned for me to squeeze into the tiny space between the table and the seat. I climbed up on my knees and bent forward with one hand on the wall of the RV, one on the top of the seat.

"Where?" I bobbed my head up and down to look through all the gaps in the blinds. No cows. Falcon was insane.

The RV left the highway and we passed a huge wall mural that said *Welcome to Jackson*. Wow, we'd driven all the way to Mississippi while I slept? I shifted my weight as the brakes squealed and compressed air escaped from somewhere.

The warmth of Falcon's hand at my hip seeped through the fabric of my PJs, and the heat of his body hit my butt. "There." He curled around me from behind and moved my hand up farther on the wall, causing me to bend deeper in the seat. His groin rubbed my ass.

While Falcon exemplified every girl's dream of a sexy bad boy, and I technically wasn't *with* Torrez, Falcon didn't spark my plugs half as much as Torrez. Like a smoking hot older brother, I liked him, but the chemistry didn't exist. "Listen, Falc— "

A whoosh of air blew across my back, and Falcon's fingers tightened on my hips before they scraped away. I turned to see Falcon on his back, Torrez on his knees with a fist pulled back, and his elbow across Falcon's throat.

With a primal grunt, Falcon grabbed the fist headed for his face and twisted to gain the advantage. He straddled Torrez for a split second before they whirled to the side and banged into the cabinets. A blur of jeans, T-shirts, and tattoos tumbled in the narrow kitchen aisle like two boulders in a rockslide.

I didn't know for sure, but I think I heard Torrez call Falcon crazy in Spanish, which would be accurate.

Then I heard something that sounded like Falcon insulting Torrez' mother.

"Uh. Stop." My first attempt to speak came out much too soft to be heard. They slammed into the wall again. "Knock it the hell off!"

They paused and leered up at me like I'd interrupted them playing rugby.

"Stop fighting. It's stupid. Just talk it out." Torrez tilted his head and Falcon drew his brows so high he made wrinkles in his forehead. Two confused puppies listening to their master's voice. "You know, use your words? Kindergarten 101?"

"Yes, let's have words." Torrez struck a sucker punch to Falcon's jaw. Falcon growled, and their fists started pummeling again. They ended up on their knees, crashing down next to my feet. I screamed and jumped back. They stopped fighting and glanced at me.

Torrez climbed to his feet and stumbled backward, holding his side, his eyes checking me out head to toe. When he saw I wasn't hurt, he said to Falcon, "Ela é minha."

That sounded like *she is mine*. Oh my goodness.

Falcon stood up and breathed heavily as he leaned against the wall. He looked like a rabid beast with his hair covering his face. "What's that? I can't understand your fucked up Spanish."

"Portuguese, fucker." Torrez braced one hand on the driver's seat and pointed to the door. "We're in Jackson. Falcon's getting off here."

Falcon chuckled as he pulled his hair back and twisted. It miraculously stayed in place. "Hey now. She has a bodacious ass, but that little rub-a-dub-dub wasn't nearly enough to get me off."

Torrez gritted his teeth at Falcon's joke, and I held back my laugh. "You're not getting off *in here*. You're getting off *the rig here*, idiot."

"You're going on without me?" Falcon sounded like the kid in the PE class lineup who wasn't picked for the team.

"Yep." Torrez stepped in front of me and crossed his arms as he tilted his head to the door.

Falcon smirked at him, not moving for the door. "You cut me off, I lose out on a fat per diem."

"I asked for transport. I didn't order a man."

"But you need one." Falcon glanced at me and his voice became caring and persuasive. "Maybe two or three. You're being tracked by two powerful groups who want to kill you."

"Groups want to kill you?" I asked. "We need two or three men?" This kept getting scarier.

Torrez held a finger up for me to wait. "I'll tell you later." He scowled at Falcon. "I can handle it alone."

"Where will you go?" Falcon's voice challenged Torrez.

"I don't know," Torrez answered deadpan.

"You should go through Mexico. Greco's hitmen won't cross into Reynosa territory. If you don't wanna be found, the belly of Mexico is the best place to hide."

Torrez relaxed his stiff arms and rubbed his chin with his thumb. "It's risky." The tension over the fight forgotten, these two military men had shifted into tactical mode.

"Hitmen?" I asked. Oh my god, actual hitmen after us?

"If you know the right places to go, follow the customs, you'll be fine. I'll send you through my hometown." Falcon kept talking as if I hadn't spoken.

"Your hometown safe?" Torrez asked.

"What is safe? Safety is an illusion. The chances of getting killed don't matter because you only need that one shot and you're dead. You stay clear when shit goes down, you're safe."

Torrez rubbed his palms over his cheeks. "I'm getting a vibe off you, you're being genuine."

"Oh, friend. I feel sad. I thought you trusted me."

"Don't trust anyone I haven't served next to in combat."

"Rogan sent me. He can attest to the many times over the last fifteen years I got his ass out of enemy fire. Without me, he'd be a bucket of bullets."

"Never served with Rogan, but—"

"Do not go there." Falcon got his face up in Torrez', so close I'm sure Torrez could taste the alcohol reeking off Falcon. "Rogan and Z Security are a class act. My brother, my friend, would lay his life down for any one of us. He's also a damn straight shot, so I wouldn't be putting him down unless you'd like to test his aim with your forehead."

Torrez rolled his eyes and pushed Falcon back. "You interrupted me. I never served with Rogan, but Dallas vouched for him, and I watched him in action at Dallas's wedding. It's obvious he has his shit together. The work Z Security is doing has been noticed. He's earning a rep as the best. So I trust him, and if he sent you, I'd expect he had a good reason."

Falcon nodded. "That reason being I know you can disappear in Mexico. No one better at staying off the grid than me."

Torrez stared out the door to the RV and squinted like he was envisioning us in Mexico. I'd never been there. "It might be crazy enough to work. Greco and Yegor would be out of their league in the heat of Mexico."

"Exactly. I would never send your Teimosa into harm's way."

Torrez turned his gaze to mine and a warm tingle went through me. Was I his Teimosa?

Falcon pulled a map from the glovebox and circled something. "Nuevo Laredo by the Texas border. Tell them Primitivo Borrego de la Cruz sent you." Falcon snapped the pen closed and drew his shoulders back. "Keep Soraya under control."

"I can take care of myself." I didn't need supervision like a child.

"I'll manage her," Torrez replied. "Now get the hell off my rig. Whether we head to Mexico or not, your ugly mug isn't invited."

"Let me grab my gear. Rogan will send you a bill for a flight back to North Carolina. And I fly first class."

"As long as your butt is off this bus, I'll pay whatever it takes."

Falcon reached into a small closet next to the bathroom and came out with an olive green duffle bag over his shoulder. "Hasta luego." He tipped his head to me as he walked to the door. "Be safe."

A twinge of sadness passed through me at Falcon leaving. I didn't get to know him very well, but being around him brought out adventurous and daring parts of my personality. "Bye, Falcon. And uh, thank you. For the RV. And for traveling this far with us. I had a good time."

Falcon and Torrez chuckled as they shared a fist grab and a bro hug. They nodded one last time like all was forgiven and the door snapped shut behind Falcon.

Chapter 11

As Falcon's larger-than-life presence left the tiny space, the wrath of Torrez the bull quickly exploded into the void.

His sinister glare locked me in place. I took a step back and my calves hit the seat cushion. He stalked toward me with his hands curling into fists.

"Now listen, Torrez. Nothing happened. He was playing around." I scrambled behind the table.

His jaw jutted forward and his nostrils flared. "I don't like other people playing with you."

"Oh."

"I am the only one who plays with you." He reached the table and stopped. "Come out from behind there."

"No thanks. I'm good right here." The ceiling of the RV forced my neck to bend at an awkward angle.

"Come over here."

"You're scaring me." And turning me on. But I didn't let him know that.

"I won't hurt you. You had fun with Falcon. Bow it's my turn to play." His big arms widened, and his fists wrapped around the edges of the table. The floor cracked and creaked as he hoisted it up and tossed it to the floor. The crash made me jump and bang my head on the roof.

"Ouch!"

A tug on my arm knocked me off balance. The ceiling and floor spun. My stomach hitting his shoulder forced a grunt from deep in my throat. Through the curtain of my hair, his ass came into view. Gorgeous as it was, I didn't want to be carried right now. I worked a hand free and slung it around to punch him in the lower back. My fist bounced off the rock hard curve of his spine. Was any part of this man soft?

"Decided something. 'Bout time I share it with you." He started talking, but I had no idea what he meant. The room spun again, and g-forces pummeled my stomach. My head bounced off the pillow I'd been sleeping on just minutes before.

Mornings suck. I shoulda stayed in bed. "Are you talking to me now or just rambling to yourself?"

He stood at the end of the bed, his chest heaving, his eyes drilling into me. "I'm talking to you, so listen up. Slept next to you last night while Falcon drove."

Oh. So it wasn't a dream? "I thought it was a dream."

"No dream. Held you in my arms while you slept deep. Probably one of the most real nights I've ever had." He crawled up on the bed and poled his arms next to my head. "Want more of that. Want my life to be real for the first time."

The heat of his body surrounded me like a cage. "Your life has never been real?"

"Not until now. I was either fighting to survive, which is not a normal state of reality for most people, or pretending to be someone I didn't wanna be."

"Who—"

His lips crashing down on mine silenced me. He growled as he lowered his hips and pressed a huge erection between my legs. Darn. Darn. Why did he have to feel so good? He stopped to nip my lower lip and tease my mouth open. This was my last chance to get out from under him, but I didn't say anything. The pull toward him overwhelmed me and surpassed all logic. With the intense passion bombarding me, and his gorgeous eyes molten on me, I didn't stand a chance. My body ached for everything he offered.

Like my head on the pillow wasn't enough for him, he planted an elbow on the bed and curled his hand around my neck. He lifted my head, pushing me into an open-mouthed kiss.

His other hand roamed over the silk of my PJs. He ended the kiss, his lips moving up my cheek. "Teimosa." He spoke so smooth and breathy. Not fair. Too sexy. With the heat of him over me, his lush lips on my skin, and the beautiful way in which he spoke, I wouldn't be surprised if I spontaneously combusted on the spot.

He reached up and pulled on something. "I knew it."

"What?" I struggled to see over my head.

"Falcon pimped us out with gear."

Arching my neck and turning my body, I saw him digging inside a compartment built into the wall at the top of the bed. "Body armor, right?"

"No. Restraints and toys."

"So like what? You could torture the bad guys with games if you catch them?"

"Nope. So I can tie you up and tease the hell outta you right now." His eyes turned devious like he was plotting my demise as he sorted through a jumble of ropes and leather bands. "You up for a serious reality check?"

"What did you have in mind?" I had an idea, but I needed to hear it from him.

"Let me bind your limbs." He held up a length of thick canvas rope. "You relax and stop thinking all the fucked up shit swirling around in there." His fingers caressed across my temple and curled into my hair behind my ear. "I'll take over for a while. At the end, you'll be so lost in the physical reality of right here and now, you'll forget your worries."

Oh my. That sounded wonderful, but... "I don't have any worries."

"You mean you're not thinking about Yegor or Greco finding us? Not scared shitless you're falling in love with me and you're not sure you can trust me?"

I shook my head, but he was right.

"You're terrified."

I nodded.

"Arms up. I'll make you trust me."

Should I do this? I could fall deeper for Torrez. Possibly beyond the point of no return. I'd never been tied up. I'd never had kinky sex. Shoot, I'd never even had good sex before Torrez. But I wanted it. I'd fantasized about a take-charge man testing my boundaries like he was suggesting. My legs shook and I grew even more wet between my legs. My body had already agreed before my mind could protest.

I stared into the emerald light of his eyes and slowly raised my arms over my head.

He grinned. "Good choice." He bent and kissed me, sensual and passionate. Yes, I'd made a good choice. Torrez would show me things I'd always dreamed of doing. Somehow, while we were kissing, he'd worked open the buttons of my top. He slipped the sleeves down my shoulders, and I arched my back to help him get it off me.

"Shit. Fuck." He groaned and stared at my naked breasts.

"Is something wrong?" I asked him

"No, God, no. I just need to pace myself."

He sucked my nipple into his mouth, biting down just enough to feel good and hurt at the same time. His other hand massaged my breast, tweaking and flicking my nipple, sending lightning spears jolting through my body.

"Pick up the pace." My hands came down and squeezed his ass.

"No. We need this. You need to trust me." He sat back and worked off my pajama bottoms and underwear. "Legs spread."

I hesitated. He pulled off his shirt and oh my lordy lordy, yes. My legs spread wide of their own will.

I lost sight of him as he wrapped a silk blindfold over my eyes and tied a snug knot. He straddled my chest, and I felt the fly of his pants brush my lips as the rope worked around my wrist. He yanked it tight and pulled my arm taut. I bit him through his pants and he groaned. "Woman."

He tied my other arm and each of my ankles. I was spread wide open for him.

"At anytime you feel uncomfortable, say *cows on my side*."

I sputtered a laugh. "Seriously?"

"Yep. You say it, I untie you and we talk it out. I won't be angry. Get it?"

"Got it."

"Good. Fuck, you look unbelievable like this. My dick is screaming to be inside you, but first..."

A thud hit my hip and trailed away. It didn't hurt. It was soft, like leather. Or suede?

"What was—"

"Relax. It's a flogger. I won't hurt you. Just focus on the spots where it hits your skin."

Another thud on my hip and the caress over my skin. Yes, definitely suede. Too smooth to be leather, it left behind a soft tingle.

"Okay?" he asked.

"Yes, more." I bent one knee as far as I could and lifted my hips from the bed. His hand on my stomach forced me back down. I bit my lip and held my breath as swipe after swipe hit every inch of my abdomen. He moved it ever so slightly each time, precise and methodical from left to right. The rhythm remained steady and relaxed, totally controlled by Torrez.

He increased the speed and pressure as he progressed lower, and by the time he reached the apex of my thighs, I squirmed and wiggled, begging him to do it *there*.

Maddeningly, the next round of swashes hit my upper thigh and trailed down my leg. He even tenderized my toes.

He moved up the other leg and closer to my inner thigh. If he skipped my clit again, I was going to have to say *cows on my side* so I could strangle the bastard.

His progress halted just below my sex with alternating swats on my inner thighs. So close.

"Please, please." I was an incoherent mess.

"You feeling your reality right about now?" He'd been quiet but his voice came out hoarse.

"Yes, yes, please."

"This is your reality, babe. I'm here. I can do this to you. Only me. Hot as hell, isn't it?"

"Yes, please. Keep going. Higher. I want to feel it."

The flogger stopped.

"No! Don't stop."

"Adding a dimension for you."

Hmm? What dimension? I gasped as his hand came down over my pussy. Two fingers probed inside and curled up. His mouth hit my tit. He bit and growled with my nipple between his teeth until it was a rigid nub. I was so turned on, I couldn't breathe or speak. All I could do was wait for Torrez to give me whatever the next layer would be.

His mouth pulled away and something tightened around my nipple.

"Oh god. Oh god. What is that?" A sting radiated from my nipple straight to my clit.

"Clothespin."

His hand kept working down below as his teeth teased my other nipple to a peak. I anticipated the sting of the second clothespin, but it still hurt.

He withdrew his fingers, and I heard a sucking sound. God, I wanted to see him licking me off his fingers like an ice cream cone. I thrashed my head, trying to dislodge the blindfold covering my eyes.

The feel of his body left me except for a point on my shins where his pants rubbed my leg. He was straddled over me, no doubt looking down on me trussed up and pinned.

I held my breath and listened to him take in two deep sucks of air, waiting to see what would happen next. The soft suede of the flogger snapped the side of my left breast and the drag jostled the clothespin, sending a tantalizing pleasure through me and ratcheting up my desperation.

The ropes pulled taut and clinched my wrists as I groaned and writhed. He hit the other breast and dragged the tassels over the clothespin, which tugged and stung my nipple in the most delicious tease ever. Fire tickled my skin everywhere. He'd left magical flames burning in my soul.

"That's it, Teimosa. Feel it."

The first strike of suede on my clit made me scream. I couldn't control it. The unexpected swat and the following caress felt phenomenal. The wetness between my legs leaked down to my ass. I was dripping wet for him, and he had a bird's eye view of it all while I suffered blindly through the deluge of his touch.

He hit my left breast again, then the right, then my clit. Torrez repeated his circle of torture.

Nipple, nipple, clit.

Nipple, nipple, clit.

"Mercy," I said, breathless.

Nipple, nipple, clit.

"Mercy."

The flogger and its whooshing noise ceased, his panting the only sound in the room. "You callin' cows?" His voice shook like glass over hot coals, barely restrained.

"No, just please. Let me come. I'm dying for it."

Finally, he grunted and answered my pleas. The flogger pounded my sex hard. Slow at first, but increasing to an unbearable pace. He was a master conductor and I was his orchestra. At least ten quick lashes in a row hit me directly on my sensitive nub.

Heaven. Nirvana. I'd found nirvana.

He changed the motion so it hit my sex once. When the wet strands returned to pounding my clit, I cried out.

"I'm gonna... I can't..."

"Yes, babe. You're magnificent. Let me see you come."

His strained voice, the pressure on my nipples from the jiggling clothespins, the relentless flap of the flogger, the whirring sound of Torrez playing me like a Stradivarius. It all overtook me and I was gone.

Holy shit. My stomach contracted, my pussy clenched.

Like nothing I'd ever felt before, a force propelled me into the cosmos, catapulting around like a meteor. Yes, yes. Nirvana.

I gulped in air, my chest heaving. Suddenly, I needed him closer. He felt so far away.

"Torrez. Now. Need your cock in me now."

"Wait."

"I can't wait."

"Next level."

A pointed object with a round end massaged my opening. It couldn't be his dick because it was much too small.

"Is it a dildo?"

"Butt plug. A small one." He skimmed it down between my cheeks and pushed it against my back opening. "First step to me fucking your ass."

"Oh my god." It felt good. I was too far gone to feel embarrassed about that.

"Relax."

"Take the blindfold off."

His fingers worked the knot, and as he came into view, I discovered he'd already removed his pants and was hovering over me naked. Thank the angels and the leprechauns, he intended to fuck me soon! His cock pointed at me from between his legs where he was kneeling and working a plug into my ass. Spectacular.

If I could paint, I would make a portrait of it. But I sucked at painting. Maybe I'd have it commissioned? No, I'd just remember this moment forever.

My head flopped back and I relaxed. The plug popped in place and created a foreign full feeling. After a few seconds, I adjusted and it felt great. I loved it.

"Now, Teimosa. Now it's time." He spoke as he untied one foot, then the other but left my hands above my head. I wrapped my legs around him. His tip teased my entrance. He slammed into me with a grunt. The fullness expanded beyond comprehension.

"Minha." He growled into my neck. I kissed his cheek until he turned his head to mine and our lips locked in a deep kiss. His chest pushed the clothespins down, and they tweaked my nipples. He pummeled into me, each stroke hitting my G-spot and my clit at the same time. And something in my ass I never knew was there. Another climax grew deep and came on fast.

"Again, babe, again."

My orgasm ripped through me. He planted his cock to the base and groaned a loud long moan into my mouth. I imagined swallowing his energy as if he was coming in my mouth.

We froze like that for a long time, heaving and coming back to the stratosphere.

He was the first to manage words. "Fuck." The awe in his tone was obvious.

"Yeah."

That about summed it up. Torrez and I were astronomical together. We couldn't deny it.

He untied my arms and rubbed my wrists. My nipples stung as he released the pins. He sucked them each in turn gently.

He trailed kisses between my breasts, up my neck, to my lips. "That was real."

"Yes. Couldn't think of a better reality."

He pulled out and situated me to his side with my head on his chest, one arm around my back, and my hand resting on the Brazilian flag on his sternum. "Let's lie here for a bit, then get some grub and hit the road again." The lazy rumble of his voice massaged my ear.

"Okay." I smiled and closed my eyes.

"See. Your fear is gone."

"Yeah."

"Anytime you feel scared, let me know, and I'll hook you up with some ultimate reality."

"Mmm." Deep in the recesses of my mind, a tiny voice protested. But for the life of me, I couldn't think of one reason why I should say no to Torrez. If there were more reality sessions in store for me, I'd be insane to turn him away.

Chapter 12

―――

"Oh my word, that was divine." My hand circled my big belly, bloated with hubcap-sized red-velvet pancakes from the Stuffed Pig Country Diner in Jackson. Leaning back in the passenger seat, I turned my head to Torrez at the wheel and felt the thoroughly-fucked smile return to my face.

He threw me the same smug grin he'd worn all through breakfast. "You love my cock."

"I meant the pancakes."

"You meant riding the bull."

"I did not."

"Admit it. This morning was the best sex you've ever had."

I laughed. No point in denying it. "By a long shot." Torrez was a beast in bed. Taking charge, exuding confidence, teasing me to the bitter edge. He'd lit flames in every crevice of my skin. The total acceptance I felt rolling off him made it even better. He wasn't judging me for what we did. He was proud of me, and he made it clear he enjoyed it too.

He started the engine, and we glided out of the parking lot. "No one's ever given you what you truly need?"

Uh-oh. This just wandered into dangerous territory. If Torrez called me a slut again now, after all we'd been through, it would hurt too much. "Let's not talk about that."

A serious frown replaced his confident grin. "Have you slept with anyone besides Yegor?"

Desperate to change the subject, I punched the screen for the music, switching out the blues he'd been playing for anything else. A rap song I happened to know came on. "This is my jam! Yo, yo, gangsta rap in da house!"

He cast me a sideways glance and smothered a laugh as he turned the radio off. "That's so not your jam. Why're you shutting down?"

I looked back at him and took in his handsome profile. "I'm afraid you'll judge me. Again."

He kept his eyes on the road. "I apologized for that. Sounds like you need to hear it again. I'm sorry. You know I'm not that guy."

I wanted to believe him, and so many signs pointed to the fact he could be compassionate and selfless. "So why'd you say those things? Your ex did a number on you that makes you distrust women?" It must've been really bad to make him think the worst of me.

"She did several numbers on me. A Vegas revue has less numbers than the crap she pulled." We passed out of the small Mississippi town and accelerated onto a two-lane highway lined with tall trees. Dark clouds filled the horizon, but it wasn't raining yet.

"Tell me about her." I wanted to hear it, and it would distract him from asking about my sexual history.

"It's a long story."

"We have endless road ahead of us. Are we stopping anytime soon?"

"No."

"Then start talking. You thought I was like her?"

"For a brief moment, I thought you were working me like she did so often. I was wrong. I shouldn't have assumed to understand your situation or motivations. I should've trusted the real you I saw inside."

That was nice and made me feel somewhat better about what happened. "So what did she do?"

"She got pregnant, racked up a huge debt, and sucked me into doing business with Greco."

Oh. I didn't expect his ties with Greco to be related to his ex-wife. "How so?"

"We were dating. I was set to leave for deployment. A week before my go date, she's crying over a positive pregnancy test. Saying it was mine. I was actually happy. Always wanted to be a dad. Woulda liked to get to know her first, but I did the right thing and married her. I left the next week and didn't even get to see my son until he was six months old."

I didn't realize Torrez had a son. "What's his name? How old is he now?"

"Drew. He's sixteen. He's an amazing kid. Looked just like me so I knew he was mine. He's got my drive. Wanted to ride a sheep when he was two years old." He chuckled and shook his head.

"Did you let him ride a sheep?"

"Yep. He was good too. Took his falls like a champ. I taught him to ride and rope. He's getting real serious about it now. I hooked him up with the best trainers in the rodeo industry. He rides calves on the junior circuit. He wants to go pro."

His son sounded brave like him. "And you want that too?"

"Fuck no. I'd like to see him take a desk job, but Lavonte blood runs in his veins. He'll never choose the safe road. I'm proud as hell of him and I support him. Pay those trainers to teach him safety mostly. He's got natural flair. Even if he doesn't go pro, he'll learn courage and determination and how to take a hoof to the balls."

I could tell by his voice he adored his son. "So where does Greco come in?"

"Two weeks after I get home on leave, she tells me she's pregnant again. In the same sentence, she tells me she spent all our money while I was gone. Every penny I sent her she blew on spa days, expensive purses, plastic surgery. While I was in the desert fighting for my life, she was here bleeding me dry."

Ooh, I was not liking this woman and the way she manipulated him when he had important duties with the Navy and probably his own stresses related to those duties. "So what did you do?"

"She introduced me to Greco. Said he'd hire me to work construction for him. I thought the guy looked shifty, but I needed cash for two kids in a hurry. I was between deployments and the pay was great. I dug us out of the hole in about six months. Good thing too cuz my daughter came early."

"She did?"

"Yeah."

The threatening rain started pounding the windshield. The pavement darkened as Torrez flipped the wipers on. "I know what you're thinking. She's not mine. I'll tell you I do not care. Peyton is mine. She's my girl. She's not Greco's and he'll never get to her."

"How old is she?"

"Fourteen. Beautiful girl. Cheerleader. Straight *A* student. Does all kinds of charity work."

"So what happened with Greco?"

"I was set to deploy again. Peyton was three months old. Caught Jacqueline in bed with Greco."

"Oh no."

"It got ugly."

"I'm sure."

"In the end, Greco had me by the balls. Said he'd claim both my kids as his. Take them into his crooked family."

"No!"

"He offered me a deal. I launder money through a construction business he'd front the money to start, he leaves my kids alone."

"So you agreed?"

"Yes. Had no choice."

"And you've been laundering money for him all this time?"

"Yeah. At first I stayed on with the SEALs, not wanting to give up my training and hard-earned position because of Greco and Jacqueline. But she kept spending every dime I made, and he kept offering me more money. So, I retired and grew Bravo Construction into Bravo Development Corporation. Been outta the Navy for ten years now. Divorced for nine."

He gave up his career for his kids, and all because of his ex-wife. "And did he leave your kids alone?"

"For the most part. He threatens to track them down every time I try to get out of our deal. But he can't find them, so he burns my places down."

"He can't find them?"

"Nope. Jacqueline moves all the time. I gotta follow her around to see my kids."

"Do you know where they are now?"

"Texas, outside Galveston."

"Oh. Is that why you spend time there?"

"Yep."

"Wherever she settles, I buy property nearby and build a house on it. I watch over her till she spooks again then I gotta chase her down again. I'll do anything for those kids. They know it too. They started calling me now and telling me when they move."

"That's good. So you have a close relationship with them even though she tried to keep them from you?"

"Yes. And that's where you enter the picture."

We came out from under a cloud and the rain stopped. "Me? I'm in the picture?"

His eyes cut to mine and I felt it deep. "You changed the whole picture."

My stomach twisted and spirals of hope sprouted up. "I did?"

"Made it beautiful."

I was part of his picture? And I made it beautiful? "Not sure I'm following you."

"Up until now, I never had a compelling reason to make running worth it. I kept women at a distance. Not wanting to drag anyone into my shit. Also not willing to risk getting duped again like I did with Jacqueline."

"You didn't have a girlfriend?"

"Nope."

"Weren't you lonely?"

"I had women I had sexual arrangements with. Took off some of the edge. But yeah, now that we're being honest. I was lonely." He reached over and brushed his knuckles down my cheek. "Missed having someone to talk to like this. Sharing my life."

All this stuff seemed very serious. We were on the run together in an RV. We'd had great sex a few times, but Torrez talked like it was so much more. I felt it too, but didn't trust it because I didn't know if I could trust him. "Am I sharing your life?"

"I'd like you to. After this morning, I'm excited as fuck. I didn't expect that from you, but you obviously like to play, so we can do that again."

"Oh we can? Can we?" He made it sound like it was my idea and he was entertaining my kinks. I had nothing to do with it. That was all Torrez and what he wanted to do to me.

"I sure as shit want to. Every chance we get to stop."

Me too. "Do I get to learn how to use a flogger?"

"On yourself?"

"No, on you."

"Nah. I don't switch." He sounded a little offended that I asked.

"How about clothespins on your nipples?" I decided to push him.

"No." He cringed and looked at me like I was crazy.

I laughed. "Why not? You can dish it out but you can't take it?"

"In the bedroom, I'm in charge. You wanna be on top, ride me hard, I'd love every second of it. But you're not tying me up or putting anything up my ass."

My laugh bellowed through the cabin. "C'mon, Torrez. Let me put a plug up your ass. It'll be hot."

"No."

"Never?"

"Never." His voice was stern, no joking.

"Darn." It would be fun to turn the tables on him, but I guess that wasn't happening.

"We're getting off topic here. You know who you're dealing with now. I want you in my life. Want you to be my shotgun rider."

I had to swallow the lump in my throat. Torrez was saying a lot of things I'd always wanted to hear. He was being honest with me. Too honest. I felt like running from it. "I need some time to think on it."

"Can give you that. We got time."

It all seemed too incredulous to believe. "You never wanted this with anyone else?"

"Nope. Just you."

"Why?" I'd thought he was phenomenal from the start. Handsome, strong, brave, funny. I was drawn to him right away. But I didn't know what he saw in me.

"Knew from the first night. The way you flirted with me like a big goof and covered it up with your practiced social presence. The way you go wild and let loose when we fuck." His smile spread a sweet warmth through my body. "Despite all you've been through, you've got an innocence about you, makes me wanna be the man to give you what you need. I could make you very happy."

The glow of his kind words jumbled with the confusion and fear brewing inside me. We'd completely passed out from under the storm, and now cottony white clouds filled the horizon. My heart wanted to believe it was a sign. That it would be safe to go all in with Torrez and enjoy the ride. The logical part of my brain kept saying he was still a criminal, he'd technically kidnapped me, and I could get hurt. By him or the people he associated with. He'd already said I was at risk because I was with him. I just didn't have enough information to make sense of all this.

"I can see you're still worried. I'll take you out tonight. We're heading to Biloxi, the mini-Vegas of the South. It'll be our second date."

That got my attention. "Ooh, I heard about Biloxi on the news. Hurricane Katrina blew the riverboat casinos out of the water."

"Yeah, they were hit hard, but they've rebuilt bigger and better. We're going to give their recovery efforts a little boost."

"Really?"

"Yep. We'll stop and get a car first."

"A car?"

"We're not rollin' up to a high-stakes casino in an RV. We'll arrive in style."

A high-stakes casino and a stylish car? Oh that sounded nice. My worries evaporated thinking about what dress I could wear for our second official date.

"And Soraya?"

"Yeah?" Our gazes locked, his green eyes growing soft and warm.

"This morning? Best I ever had. By a long shot."

Chapter 13

T *orrez*

The McClaren handled like a dream down the strip in Biloxi, Mississippi. So precise and responsive. Combine the luxurious new leather smell with the perfume coming off Soraya, driving the vehicle was sensory overload and a total turn on.

I wanted to get the graphite gray, but my girl has a thing for red so we ended up with the volcano red 12C Spider. Now that we were cruising in it, I saw her point. The red is superior to the other colors and adds to the driving high. All my life I chose gray, blend in. Time to choose red.

My fingers inched up her thigh, and my pinky tickled her panties under her skirt. Her legs shivered, and she gave me a contented smile. Much better reaction than the last time I touched her there.

"Did I tell you you look breathtaking in that dress?" I did not lie. The stretchy mesh fabric hugged her curves like the Spider hugged a turn. The cranberry red dress had long sleeves and a conservative neckline, but she might as well have been naked. Black leather straps spaced a few inches apart provided the only discretion. The strategic strap over her chest barely covered the nipple. She'd chosen the black heels with a chain buckle above her ankle before our little bondage session. Soraya had it in her the whole time. I just brought it out to play.

"A few times." The three inches of bangles on her arms slid down as she reached for the silver hoops in her ears. The guys called those hooker hoops. Pull her legs up and hook her heels in them as you fuck her. She'd also chosen to wear the diamond collar I'd bought for her. She may not have been aware of it, but that necklace declared her as *mine*.

"I'll say it one more time. Too damn hot. I shoulda fucked you first to take the edge off."

She chuckled. "That wouldn't work."

She was getting to know me. "Nope. As long as you're wearing that, my dick's never gonna settle." My thumb traced the bumps of the diamonds around her neck.

She turned toward me and waggled her eyebrows, the tip of her tongue peeking out between her lips. "Let's skip the casino then and just get a room." Man, her mix of seductive and goofy totally worked on me.

"Tempting. Very tempting." I liked that I'd broken through to her, and she felt comfortable enough to take the initiative. "But no. Need to blow through some cash first."

"Why are we spending money like water again?"

Telling her this would probably frighten her, but she needed to know the truth if she chose to stay with me. "After we saw him at the restaurant, Greco transferred ten million dollars into my account. It's dirty. Drug money. Blood money. He expects me to give him five mil back clean. I'm done dancing with Greco.

I'm going legit and disposing of the evidence. No place better to unload cash than a casino."

She frowned and chewed her lower lip. "He's not going to like you spending his money."

"Nope. That's why we're running."

She looked down, the seriousness of our current reality scaring her again. "What about your kids?"

Good question. "I beefed up security on their place in Texas, but he wants me this time."

That seemed to make her more concerned. "And you don't care if he burns your place down?"

"No."

"Why?"

"My home is with you now." She blushed like she did whenever I gave her the truth direct and unfiltered. "Wherever you are, there I am. Home. Don't need four walls."

My hand slid up into her hair to guide her face to mine for a brief kiss as we turned right into the roundabout outside the Paradise Casino. The valet's eyes lit up like he'd been waiting his entire life to drive a McClaren.

I pulled up to his kiosk and cracked the window. "I'll park it."

His smile froze as the light in his eyes faded. "Oh sure. Sure. Park it right here." He pointed to a spot right in front, but I took one on the end. If we needed to get out fast, we'd be clos-est to the exit. A twisted urge deep inside me hoped we'd be forced to leave in a hurry so I'd have a valid reason to see what the car could do.

The engine cut out, the doors swung forward and up, and I ex-ited the car like a driver at Daytona. I walked around the back and offered her a hand. Totally caught a glimpse of red under-wear as she poked one leg out and let me help her from the low seat. She wobbled in her heels as she smoothed her dress down and peered around the entrance to the casino. A tiny worry wrinkle formed on the bridge of her nose. Cute. She wanted to wear that outfit, but was insecure about it.

"I'm gonna be the proudest man that ever lived, walkin' in there with you on my arm."

She perked up, worry line gone, smile returned. Good girl.

We entered the lobby, both grinning big. The lights and sounds of the slots, her gorgeous body next to me, lush carpet under my new shoes. Felt like the king of the world. "Let me get some chips." We stopped at the cashier. "VIP casino please."

"Ten thousand to enter. Need your ID. Minimum bid to play, two thousand."

I heard a small gasp from Soraya.

"No problem." I handed the cashier twenty grand in hundreds and a fake ID for Ray Charles.

Her eyes widened, but she took it and started counting. Cash made everyone suspicious. Another reason to get out of the biz now.

She handed me two keycards. "The black key opens the elevator to your right and will take you to the VIP casino on the 36th floor. The white key is a complimentary room, Suite 1510."

"Can we get a room on the second floor? Afraid of heights."

"Sure." The cashier messed around with her computer. "Room 208."

My hand slipped into Soraya's like it belonged there and I led her to the elevator. As the doors closed, she asked, "You're afraid of heights?"

"Yeah."

"I thought you were a marine mammal who scaled buildings?"

"It's a very specific fear. Only in hotels in Mississippi."

She snorted as the elevator lifted us. Alone. My chance to get my hands on that dress. I pressed her up against the wall and kissed her. She responded like I wanted, kissing me back and begging for more. The mesh of the dress stretched as my hands caressed the hourglass of her waist. Too soon, the elevator dinged, and we both wiped her lipstick off our lips.

We stepped out into the foyer of a casino much fancier than the one downstairs. No slots. No garish lights. Chandeliers and black velvet. A rich man's den of doom.

A hostess wearing a glimmering silver gown came up and offered us champagne. Soraya took a glass. "Can I get you anything, sir?"

Soraya edged closer to me and pressed her tits to my bicep.

No worries, baby. Everyone here can see I'm with you. She's no threat.

"Caipirinha."

She nodded like she was familiar with the traditional Brazilian cocktail.

Soraya's mouth gaped open as she took in her surroundings. Not what I expected from a princess. "Yegor didn't take you out at all?"

"No. We only attended school and made appearances for his oil associates. The rest of the time we worked long hours at headquarters."

I squeezed her hand and squashed what I wanted to say about Yegor and the way he treated her. "I'll show you then. Let's start with roulette."

The dealer nodded to us as we approached the table. A man with groomed gray hair and old wise eyes. They put their most experienced dealers up here. I glanced up at the security camera. Hopefully no one here would recognize me.

"Kiss for luck." I held two thousand dollar chips up to Soraya's lips. She gave them a soft kiss, and my eyes lingered there for a moment. Damn she had kissable lips. "Red." I placed the chips on the table.

The ball spun and popped and finally settled. "Red. Winner."

Shit. Wanted to lose here.

"Don't kiss this one," I whispered in her ear and placed ten chips on red.

"Why?" she asked.

I kissed her ear, and she shivered as I spoke low and quiet. "Trying to lose."

She scrunched up her nose at me. "Why? Winnings are yours to keep. Greco's money was spent at the cashier."

"Shh." I pressed a finger to her lips. "You're right. But be quiet. Don't want to draw any attention."

She licked my finger. "Shoot, Torrez, you in that tailored suit and me with my hair all big, you had to know it was going to draw attention."

"I wanted to take you out. Wouldn't change tonight for anything."

"Red. Winner!" The dealer pushed a boatload of chips my way.

Shit. We won twenty-four grand in our first two spins.

The rest of the night went on like that. We lost two rounds of poker but won big again in blackjack. "You are truly my good luck charm."

A short Chinese man in a tuxedo approached us. "Mr. Charles, I am Simon Li, manager of Club Thirty-Six." He offered me his hand and I shook it. "Congratulations on your fortuitous evening. You have won a coveted platinum chip. One hundred thousand dollar chip." He handed me an oversized chip covered in silver and diamonds. "Pose for picture on our high-roller's board?"

"No pictures." But I was too late. The waitress had already snapped a shot of Simon with Soraya and me.

"I'd appreciate if you didn't share that picture."

"Of course. No problem, sir. Please, return to your game."

He acted hospitably, but something in his eyes told me he'd recognized me. He planned to send my picture to every casino in Biloxi. Greco would know where we were within a few hours.

"In fact, we have to leave now." I grabbed my tub of chips and Soraya's hand and headed to the elevator.

"What's the matter?" she asked me as we entered the elevator. "Why're we leaving?"

"He took our picture."

"But he said he wouldn't post it."

"And you believe him? We need to get the hell out of here."

"You really think someone would find us from one picture in a casino?"

"Not taking that chance." I stopped the elevator at the second floor and guided her to Suite 208.

"I thought we had to leave."

"We have time for this."

Inside the door, my hand at the base of her back guided her to stand in the entryway. "Wait here a second." No manual locking mechanism on the interior door. One other exit. Narrow balcony. Twenty feet up. Easy jump to a grass landing. The Mc-Claren just around the corner. We were good here for a while.

Her eyes watched me take my jacket off and place it on the bed. My weapon would be close enough there if I needed it. Now what to do with my girl? She needed to understand if she wore a dress that checked all my boxes, she'd have to complete the survey. My hand in my pocket came in contact with the chip Simon had given us. Yes. The chip. Perfect for this evening.

We smiled at each other as I walked into the bathroom.

"This is a fabulous room," she said as she turned to face me.

The platinum chip turned chilly under the cold water of the bathroom faucet. Small diamonds around the perimeter sparkled in the fluorescent light. With rounded edges, it was a little larger than a regular chip.

"It is." She stepped back when I took a step closer to her. Torrez the bull had his horns out and she looked scared. I found a spot on the wall and nailed her to it with my hips. My hands roamed over the fabric of her dress and grabbed her right breast. Yes, stretchy mesh and leather straps. When our lips met, the fire smoldering between us all night burst into flames.

"This dress is lethal." I hitched the hem up above her hips. Couldn't rip it because she needed clothes in case we had to run and damn if I could figure out how to get that thing off. I dropped to my knees and inhaled her scent from between her legs.

Her thighs trembled and clenched. Her fingers scrubbed over my short hair. I wanted to dive in, and we were in a hurry, but the platinum chip was the ideal temperature to slip into the top of her panties. I made sure it landed on her clit.

She gasped. "Oh my god."

"Cold?"

"Yes."

"Let me warm it up." I opened my mouth and blew a hot breath over the chip. "Better?"

"Yes." Her hands squeezed my head and pulled me closer.

I grabbed one of her ankles and propped her thigh over my shoulder. She wavered, but my hand on her hip held her steady against the wall.

Through the fabric, my tongue played with the chip. Small circles, big circles, hard pressure, gentle pressure.

"Oh, oh, oh." Her fingernails scratched from the base of my neck to the top of my head.

That's it, baby. Man, she was exquisite when she let go like this. When her thighs tensed and her breath became ragged... I stopped.

Gritting her teeth and narrowing her eyes at me, her voice was deep. "Damn you, Torrez. Fucking tease."

I chuckled and kissed up her belly to her lips. "Want my mouth on yours when you come the first time." I slipped my hand inside her panties, swiping the chip down and dipping it in her wet cunt. "Gonna take it, inhale it, swallow it."

When the slippery chip returned to her clit, she came alive, squirming on my fingers. I kissed her and forced our tongues together, tiny whimpers escaping from deep in her throat. Delicious.

She opened her mouth in a noiseless cry as her pussy pulsed on my hand, my mouth and hand prolonging her orgasm as long as possible.

I pulled the dress up over her tits and feasted on them as I unbuckled my pants. Could not get inside her fast enough. My mouth trailed up to her ear. Her ankle pulled me closer.

"You ready?"

"Yes." Her plea was desperate. Placing the chip in my palm, I pulled down her panties and she stepped out of them. The tip of my dick found her sweet spot and worked inside.

"God, babe. So tight. Like a vise." I held the chip to her lips. "Open." She took the chip between her teeth. "Hold it there like that." She nodded. "Good girl."

No time for slow, I slammed into her. She moaned around the chip and clutched my shoulders. My orgasm came up fast. I was almost there just watching her come. My head spun and my balls drew up as I gave her everything I had, transferring all the pressure, the stress, the adoration from my heart into hers. She bit down on the chip, coming again at the same time.

As we came down from our fantastic high, I took the chip from her mouth and kissed her. I wanted to say *I love you*, but she wasn't ready. It wasn't the right time. "Fucking explosive with you."

"Yes, unbelievable." Her cheeks were flushed, her lips red and puffy, hot breaths hitting my chest where she rested her forehead.

"Could fuck you forever."

"Yes, forever." She was delirious and just repeating my words but someday she'd say forever and mean it.

I carried her to the bed, placed her relaxed body in it gently, and flopped down on top of her, my elbows bracing me over her so I could kiss her again. Maybe we could go one more round.

"Is that a vibrator in your pants?"

"No, it's my phone. But that gives me some ideas."

"Oh no, you are not using your phone as a vibrator on me."

"Why not? You might like it." I laughed and checked my screen.

Falcon: Bounty on your ass. 1 mil alive. 2 mil dead.

Shit. Greco put more money out for my dead body than a live capture? That meant he was done coercing me. He knew I was turning on him. The only way this would end was with one of us dead.

Falcon: You were spotted in Biloxi.

Fuck. Fuck me. Fuck. Goddamn Simon Li taking our picture.

"We're leaving." I buttoned my pants and pulled on my jacket.

I handed her her undies from the floor. She pulled them up and tugged her dress down. "Now? Why? Did someone see the picture?"

"Yep. Someone who wants me dead. Have you heard of fight or flight?"

"Yes."

I drew my pistol from my jacket. "Time to fly." Her hand shook in mine as she snagged her purse and followed me to the door. "Stay behind me. No matter what."

"Oh my god." She whimpered.

With a glance over my shoulder, I saw her lip trembling. "No crying. Calm down. Just keep it together till we get to the Mc-Claren."

"Mmm-hmm."

Shit. She was panicking.

I cracked the door to see two men headed our way. Helix, a bounty hunter I'd met a few times through my dealings with Greco. The machine. No emotions. Biomechanical tattoos of skin tearing open to gears, clocks, and bombs were his calling card. Helix killed unceremoniously and walked away with the cash, never a moment of human regret. The other guy with him I didn't recognize. "Two thugs in the hallway coming our way."

"How do you know they're here for us?"

"Both carrying handguns." Handguns were less powerful than rifles. They wouldn't be able to shoot through the door, but if they breached it, we were sitting ducks.

"Oh no oh my no my no my god."

Getting her out in her state would slow me down. What could I use to block the door and buy us some time? The shower head in the bathroom popped off with one strike from my fist.

"What are you... oh my god."

"It'll be fine." I punched the pipe till it pointed to the doorway. "Step back." The full-throttle spray from the pipe hit the entry door at chest level. "Perfect. Let's go."

I tugged her to the sliding glass door and out to the narrow balcony. "Get on my back."

"We're going over the balcony? How high is it?" She peered over the edge.

"Woman, get on my back."

"I— "

Helix and his buddy banged on the door. "Lavonte? You in there? Need to have a word."

Two shots hit the door from the outside. They breached the door. "Fuck." I bent and pulled her forearm over one shoulder, hoisting her up in an Army carry to the other.

The water spray hit them hard and threw them off. I had one leg over the balcony when a shot pinged off the glass of the sliding door. Another zinged over our head.

A third shot I didn't catch where it hit, but it felt close. She grunted. Oh shit.

Her death grip around my neck loosened. No.

We thunked hard on the grass, but I broke most of her fall. I pulled her into my arms and raced the twenty yards to the McClaren. Thank god they didn't fire on us as I ran. Maybe we were too visible out here or maybe they were jumping the balcony too.

I settled her in the passenger seat. Shit. Fuck. Blood. She'd been hit. I raced around the back and dove into the driver's seat. The wheels skidded before the door even lowered.

She was in shock, staring down at her chest and the crimson stain spreading near her armpit. The wheels screeched as we rounded a corner. No one could catch us in this car. No one.

"I'm bleeding."

"Where does it hurt?"

She reached for her left breast. "I don't know."

"Hang on, babe. I'll get us to a safe spot and check you."

"Okay." Her head lolled back and she was out.

"Fuck!" Goddamn mother fuckers. Shoulda killed them when they entered. Taken a defensive position. I didn't want risk it with her in the room. I thought we could make it out clean. Like they never saw us.

Holy hell. My gut twisted as I tried to think straight. Lots of blood. I needed to find the source of the bleeding and stop it.

As I looked for a place to stop, I offered up a silent prayer. It had worked for me over the years—sometimes. Not all the time, but sometimes, I received mercy and answered prayers.

Please, God. Not her. Not now. She's my girl. My future. Bring her through this safe. I've been waiting for her my entire life and I just found her. Don't take her from me. Give me one more chance. I swear I'll make it right. She'll be happy. She'll never want. Just please don't take her. I love her.

If she died, my dad was right. I was good for nothing, always running and never standing up to fight, hurting people in the process.

No. No. My dad was wrong. I'd proven myself in my career as a SEAL and over the years dealing with Greco. She would make it through this. I'd make sure of it.

Chapter 14

Soraya

Darkness. The kind of dark where your eyes never adjust no matter how hard you search.

Pain. Like a scorching branding iron to my breast.

Stop it. Stop. The pain. Make it stop. Help. Torrez?

Panic. Where is Torrez? Was he hurt? Fear pounded below the pain in my chest and constricted my throat. He couldn't be dead. I tried to call out for him but no sound formed.

A heavy thump forced my eyes open. Daylight. Suede walls. Low ceiling. Tiny windows. The familiar rocking of the RV cruising down the highway.

I was wearing my red silk PJs and lying in the bed at the back of the RV. My hand searched for the source of the pain and discovered a bandage taped to my chest above my left breast.

What happened in Biloxi? We had mind-blowing sex against the wall, and Torrez got creative with a very expensive poker chip. He received a text and jumped into action. We tried to leave, but... Oh my god, men were after us. Loud pops hurt my ears. Bullets hit the glass. Torrez jumped from the balcony like Spider-Man. In the car, blood stained my dress. Weird traces of light filled my vision. I passed out?

The bandage covered a gunshot wound?

Gritting my teeth, I threw my feet over the edge of the bed and pulled myself up. I had to see if he was okay.

The bedroom door creaked open and swung with the shaking of the bus. In the driver's seat, his muscular arm in his black tee protruded beyond the edge of the seat.

I exhaled and rested my head on the wall. He was okay. We were on the road again. Together. And his strong arms held the wheel. Driving us to safety.

Arms the size a professional wrestler would have. Arms that held me as we jumped from two stories up. Hands that had tied me up and given me more pleasure in a few days than my wildest dreams.

How could one buff arm inked in black, green, and red mean so much to me?

I didn't know where this man came from, but he'd changed me forever. I'd never been in love, but the warm glow in my heart eclipsing all the pain sure felt like what I'd seen portrayed in movies. Torrez was my leading man.

"Born to be Wild" blared from the speakers as he tapped his fingers on the steering wheel. His eyes caught mine in the rearview mirror. He turned down the volume, and his temples crinkled with his smile. "You awake, sleeping beauty?"

"I think I am." My first step without the wall's support didn't go so well. The pain caused me to wobble, and I had to grip the couch to hold me up.

"Stay there. I'll pull off the road here in a minute."

"No. Keep going. I can make it." Using the table and a few side bars, with my legs wide and awkward for balance, I made it to the front of the RV.

I lowered myself into the passenger's seat and buckled in.

"You don't need a buckle if it hurts your injury."

"I'm good." We were passing through an urban city. Bums on the street. Litter on the ground. Concrete buildings with bars over the windows.

"Twizzler?" He offered me a twisted black licorice rope from a pack in his lap as he chewed casually.

"Do you have red?"

"Nope. Red sucks. Black rocks."

"I'll try it." He handed me a piece. The gooey candy stuck to my teeth and tasted like tires. "I'll pass on the Twizzlers."

"More for me."

"It's weird," I said, not able to articulate the déjà vu the licorice stirred in me. "I've never had that candy before that I can remember. Yet I know I prefer the red."

"Maybe you saw it in a drugstore somewhere."

"No. I know how the red tastes, but I don't remember ever eating it."

He grunted. "Our subconscious remembers tastes and smells even when our conscious brain doesn't."

"Hmm. Anyway, where are we?"

"Crossing over the Rio Grande into Mexico via Laredo."

"Wow." The brakes squeaked as we came to a stop amidst a bunch of other cars being funneled over a narrow bridge.

"This doesn't make you nervous? I mean so many cars standing still on a bridge in a scary neighborhood."

"Just relax. No one will mess with us. We look like tourists."

The nagging feeling that Torrez was lying to me persisted and doubt kept creeping in. "This doesn't look safe."

"It's not if you're a drug lord or a gang member, but we should pass no problem."

"I hate to tell you this, but you look more like a drug lord than a tourist." Oh shoot. That came out totally wrong. I didn't mean to accuse him of looking like a gang member.

He stopped chewing his licorice and clenched his hands on the wheel. "You throwing low blows today? The way you take my cock, I'm thinking you like the way I look."

"I do. I'm sorry. I didn't mean it. I'm just freaking out. Why are there so many police?"

"Hotspot for trafficking cartels. Cocaine, meth, heroin, weapons. Word right now is, the Reynosa Cartel controls the bridge after the last bloodbath in Nuevo Laredo."

The last bloodbath? As if there had been many? "And why are we here?"

"Because Dubare's soldiers won't cross into Reynosa territory, even if there's a sweet bounty to be had."

"There's a bounty out on us?" He'd mentioned bounty hunters last night but it didn't register.

"Just me." He sounded so casual for a man fleeing the country because there was a price tag over his head.

"And why won't they cross the border to get you?" I was afraid to ask.

"It could spark an international war. The Dubare Syndicate keeps a healthy distance from the Reynosa Cartel. Falcon's idea was actually really good. They won't find us in the belly of Mexico's drug cartels."

He seemed way too confident. "No. But the drug dealers might find us."

"Not if we don't draw attention to ourselves." His jaw clenched and his voice scratched with irritation.

"This RV is huge! How could we not draw attention?"

"Let them come after me then. We're armed to the hilt." His nonchalance about all this grated on my last nerve.

"I don't think I can handle another gun fight."

"You're feeling scared again."

Of course I was. He expected me to sit here through all this and not be afraid? Impossible.

"I was shot!" My hands gripped the armrest to keep from slapping him.

"You were grazed by a bullet." He shrugged and sank lower into his chair. Relaxing while he talked about me getting shot!

"And you didn't take me to a hospital? Instead we're back on the road in this tank?"

"This is a lot nicer than any tank I ever drove." The condescension in his voice sent me over the edge of fury. "And I didn't take you to a hospital because I'm a trained medic. I inspected your wound, cleaned it up, and you're good to go."

"Good to go?"

"Yep."

"And this is no big deal to you? This is your reality? Drug lords and gun battles?"

"It's *our* reality. We're in this together."

Oh hell no. "What am I in, Torrez? Because I never signed up to be shot at. I don't want to take an RV through the drug center of the world."

He turned down the radio and pinned me with a glare. "If you're gonna be with me, you'll need to grow some hair on your balls. Toughen up. Fast. Don't panic like you did in Biloxi."

"I didn't panic." I thought I handled it well even though I was terrified.

"You were a bumbling mess. You shoulda jumped on my back, and you wouldn't have gotten shot."

"You don't know that." God, what an arrogant prick. I wouldn't even have been there if it weren't for him.

"I do. I've been in the exact same situation enough times to know where and when the bullets would hit. We had seconds to get out and you wasted them." He shook his head and clicked his tongue, making me feel stupid for getting shot.

"Excuse me for not keeping my calm when two thugs were shooting at me! How dare you blame me for getting shot?" My voice screeched through the cab.

"Grazed."

Oh my god. He wasn't going to take any responsibility for this? "A bullet pierced my skin! This is your fault. I would never be on the run from some crazy Mafia dude and a bunch of *hitmen* if you hadn't kidnapped me."

His eyes narrowed and turned cold. "No. You'd be at home on your knees for your prince. Bowing down and worshiping his dick."

Oh, I'd seen this Torrez before. He'd crushed my soul with his hurtful words. I should've never forgiven him.

"Shut up, you ass." I crossed my arms over my chest, but it hurt, so I gripped the armrests again. This conversation was done. I refused to utter another word.

"What's better? Living large and having earth-shattering sex or being held captive and sucking small dick?"

Okay, I had to respond to that. "*You* are infuriating."

"That the best you got? Need to teach you how to fight dirty." He chuckled as we finally inched up to the inspection point. "Quiet now. Your name's Della Robinson if he asks you."

My blood boiled at his shushing me and giving me a stupid alias.

A stocky border-patrol guard with dark glasses glared at our RV from front to back.

Torrez lowered his window and gave the officer a polite smile and two American passports. "Hola." He looked cool and calm, no hint of the fight we were having.

The guard sniffed and turned the passports over, not even looking inside. "You do not have the correct papers."

Oh no. We were going to get stopped at the border. Torrez and his stupid machismo would get us in even more trouble.

They exchanged words in Spanish, their voices deepening and ratcheting up in intensity. My heart thudded, both from the fight and the fear that we'd be spending tonight in a Mexican prison.

Torrez reached over and opened the dash. He gave the man a blank piece of paper folded around a hundred dollar bill.

A gold-toothed smile filled the guard's mouth. "Gracias." The guard pocketed the cash and nodded his head, waving us through.

We passed under the covered structure and slowly emerged onto tiny neighborhood streets. The RV barely squeezed around the turn.

I let out the breath I'd been holding. "Why didn't you just give him the cash in the beginning?"

"I had to bargain with him first to earn his respect. Then he looked like the winner when he took the cash."

"Ahh, tricky. So are we in Mexico now?"

"Yep."

The Mexican side of the Rio Grande was much more rundown than the American side. A woman sold shoes out of a dilapidated house. Shops with broken signs offered to buy gold.

My comfortable life suddenly seemed far more privileged than I'd ever realized compared to these poor families just trying to get through to the next day. I shrank back in my seat and tried to hide the shock on my face by staring out the window.

"Never been to a Mexican border town?" he asked me softly.

I shook my head. My eyes teared up. Darn it.

"You're feeling bad for them?" God, how did he read me so well?

"Yes." When my eyes closed, a tear fell and I swiped it away. "I wish I could do something. Can we spend money here like crazy to help them?"

"We can do that. I've seen poverty all across the world. It gets much worse than this."

"How do you handle it? It's so sad." I'd seen poor areas in the media and done some venturing into the run-down parts of Boston and Veranistaad, but I felt immersed in this neighborhood. Like they could be my family and their pain was my pain.

"You try to help the worst off. Stay focused on your mission. Trust everyone is on their own journey and you move on with yours. I can't save everyone." He spoke like he'd thought about it a lot.

"But you saved me?"

He pulled his gaze from the road and looked at me purposefully. God, those green eyes melted me every time. "You were not free." The compassion in his voice broke me. I didn't deserve it.

"I had a clean bed. A safe place to sleep. Fine food. I wasn't poor. Why me instead of them? It just doesn't seem fair."

"You sit down and talk to these people, most of them find a way to make the best of it. They love their families. They have faith. And they have their freedom. There's a difference between poverty and oppression. Hard to see the difference without looking deeper. I made that mistake when I met you. I saw the jewels, your beautiful makeup and hair. I knew Yegor was rolling in money. It wasn't until I talked to Zook I found out about Cecelia and made the connection you were being held against your will. Now you're free."

Free. I didn't feel free right now. "How am I free? We're on the run in fear for our lives. So bad that we'd come here to hide?"

"This is temporary."

He'd said that before. "It is? How long will we be on the run like this?"

"Till Greco is dead."

"So we're waiting for someone to kill him before someone kills us?"

"That's one way to look at it."

"Torrez."

"I'm falling hard for you, babe. Maybe already fallen. Never met a woman like you before. Sweet on the inside, stubborn outside. I knew when you swallowed your fear and walked into that casino wearing a dress you were nervous about pulling off, you were meant to be mine."

He'd basically confessed to plotting Greco's death and falling me at the same time. "This is too much. I can't..."

"I get if you're too scared to see the big picture right now, but you need to know I'm going to bust my ass to make your life golden. Once we're clear, you can be a model, an actress, whatever you want to be, but you'll be with me and you'll do it wearing my ring on your finger."

I gasped and gulped an oh my god. "Uh. So... say I buy into all this. And say for example I fall for you too..."

"You will. If you haven't already." He was so sure, but I had serious doubts.

"You've got this all planned out."

"Once the hit on me is cancelled, which it will be as soon as Greco is dead, I can concentrate on bringing Yegor and Ivan down."

"How are you going to do that?"

"Don't know yet. Plan on talking it through with Zook as soon as we're clear. Right now the biggest threat is Greco and the bounty hunter from Biloxi, Helix. I met him a few times through my dealings with Greco. He's sent Helix to threaten me more than once. I believe Helix is also the arsonist behind all my burned places."

As we drove further from the border, the streets became wider and cleaner.

"You just confessed to a lot of crimes."

His eyes locked on mine. "I didn't."

"You confessed to laundering money for the Mafia and planning to kill Greco, Yegor, and Ivan. You've made me an accomplice to murder."

"I didn't say I was gonna kill them. I said someone would kill Greco, and I'd talk to Zook about Yegor and Ivan. That is not a murder confession. I told you the truth about the money because I need you to understand me. I'm trusting you not to share that information."

"You put me in a tough situation. Being a model isn't my only career opportunity, ya know."

"What did you study at Hale?"

"Criminal justice." His eyebrows rose and his eyes filled with surprise and respect. "If I were a lawyer, I'd be obligated to report you to the authorities."

"Did you go to law school yet? Pass the bar?"

"No."

"Then you don't have to report me. Besides, you become a lawyer, I'll make you my counsel and you can't tell anyone. Attorney-client privilege."

"That's semantics and grasping at straws."

"No. It's your reality, babe. Now I want you to think hard on it because I know I did. Spent a lot of time figuring out what I wanted. For us. We have the potential to be phenomenal together. You want to go to law school, I'll make that happen. You want kids, I'm good with that too. But you and I are gonna live free and love each other. It's going to be grand. But you need to trust me. I'll keep you safe, but you gotta move when I say move. Quiet when I say quiet. And don't shiver in your boots if we find ourselves under attack again."

"You make it sound so easy, but wonderful too."

"It will be. You'll be happier than you ever dreamed. And you'll get my cock with the deal."

"You're such an ass. You think I'd risk my life for your cock?"

"You totally would. You already have. You love my reality. Just accept it."

Could I do that? Could I accept this magnificent man would love me and fulfill my heart's deepest desires? He'd already taken my body to sublime levels, and my heart pretty much confessed love for him.

But shiny objects that seemed too good to be true usually were. The truth was Torrez would hurt me like Cage, like Yegor. I'd either end up heart broken or riddled with bullets. Happy endings didn't happen for me. No. I needed to leave Torrez. It would hurt for a while, but he'd be free of me. He could kill whoever he needed to without dragging me along.

He pulled off the main road into a modern looking hotel called La Real del Nuevo Laredo. He cut the engine and turned his whole body to me. He took my hands in his. Torrez had big, warm hands. Mine were cold and small.

"I can tell you're scared, babe. I'm sorry you were hurt." One of his hands gently pressed to the bandage on my chest. "You're right. It's not your fault. It's on me. You're going to be okay. We're going to make it through this. I can't give you a reality check right now because you need to heal and I need to sleep. This is a relatively safe area. We'll get a room. I'll hold you in my arms. You'll calm down."

I seriously doubted the fear rolling in my gut would calm down anytime soon. I had no doubts panic was about to overtake me and send me spiraling out of control.

Chapter 15

Torrez

My attempts failed. Her breathing never evened out. Instead of turning and opening to me, her shoulders stayed hunched. Her face remained hidden and curled away. My words couldn't convince her to trust me. She needed actions. Lying safe in my arms in a luxury hotel wasn't enough. My Teimosa's fears clung to her like barnacles crusted on a ship's hull, slowing her down and costing her valuable fuel.

Without her confidence in me, we wouldn't make it out alive. In times like this, doubt leads to deadly consequences.

As I was thinking about decisions made in fear, she stirred. I kept my eyes closed as she inched out of the bed, checked back to see I wasn't looking, and slipped her sweet ass into her jeans. She put on a bra, T-shirt, and shoes before sifting through the bags to pull out the diamond choker and the longer chain.

She shoved them into her purse and snuck out the door without looking back.

Christ. She left me.

Where the hell did she think she was going?

I dressed and checked my weapon, giving her a head start. Let her have a minute to feel the panic of being alone in Mexico, even though she really wasn't. I'd never leave her.

How much trouble could she get into in a few minutes at two in the afternoon? Oh shit. Probably a lot. I took the stairs three at a time and stopped in the parking lot. Her long locks of chestnut hair blew behind her as she ran across—holy shit—six lanes of Highway 85. She paused at a fountain in the median and made a mad Frogger dash across the other lanes. For a girl who was supposedly scared, she had no qualms racing full-speed into traffic.

She walked through the front door of a cantina on the opposite side of the road. A handwritten sign in the window said *La Batanga*, a Mexican drink of tequila, lime, and cola. I entered behind her and pressed my back to the wall, curious what she'd say.

She glanced at the adobe walls covered with framed pictures of Mexican tequila bosses drinking batanga in the cantina. She tucked her hair behind her ears and approached the older man standing behind the bar. He appraised her from head to toe as he cleaned out a tall glass with a bar towel.

"Can I use your phone?" He raised salt and pepper eyebrows at her question. A quick perusal of the images on the walls told me he was the owner.

Two other men sat drinking beers at a table by the window. Their eyes tracked Soraya, her hair, jeans, and everything about her proclaiming her a tourist. We locked gazes and I nodded at them. They didn't acknowledge me but turned their attention back to their drinks.

"What is it you need?" The owner smiled at Soraya.

"I need to call... uh..." She looked over her shoulder and stiffened when she saw me.

"Who do you need to call?" He set the glass and towel down and stared at her.

"Uber. I need a ride."

I held back my laughter.

"Uber?"

"Uber-o. Need-o ride-o." She spoke slowly like the guy was deaf. He'd already spoken English to her. She shouldn't have insulted him by trying to add an *O* to the end of American words.

"And where would you like to go, señorita?" He offered her an amused grin, but his eyes showed him noting the unintentional slur.

She opened her purse, and all eyes fell on the jewelry sparkling inside. "El Paso."

At that, the men from the table stood up and strolled over to her. "We can take you to El Paso."

Enough letting her flounder. Time to step in. I noticed the other men move as I walked toward the bar. I stood to her right and placed a hand on her left shoulder. *Minha.*

She startled and pulled away, standing in front of the two men who had walked up.

She kept her eyes down. Couldn't look at me.

The owner addressed me in Spanish. "You know her?"

"She is mine," I answered in Spanish.

"The lady says she'd like a ride to El Paso."

"She is crazy. Forgot to take her meds today. I'll bring her back to the hotel. Sorry to bother you."

"Did you just call me crazy?" she asked with her sass on full display, no clue about the danger she was in.

"Of course not." I bent down to whisper in her ear. "Walk out slowly."

"No." She planted her feet and crossed her arms as she spoke to the owner. "If you don't have Uber, I'd like you to call me a taxi, please."

Holy shit. She was serious. She didn't trust me and wanted to leave me. "They aren't going to do that, Teimosa."

They all chuckled at me calling her scary.

Good. So far things were progressing well. I'd created goodwill by speaking Spanish and making them laugh.

"Are you with him?" the owner asked her.

This was it. Her chance to end this situation and walk out of here with her jewelry intact. The longer we talked, the greater the chance of her getting robbed or worse.

She cocked her hip and glared at me. "No."

There you go. Judas's betrayal was complete.

"She says she's not with you. So you can go."

The two men stepped around Soraya and lined up shoulder-to-shoulder in front of me.

"Not leaving." I bent my knees and braced. Adrenaline spiked through my body. If flight fails, it's fight.

The two younger guys came at me together. They went for my arms. I ducked and dodged. My punch connected with the first guy's face. My knuckles crunched. He went down, leaving me with only one opponent.

He swung, missed, and we wrestled. His arm snaked around my neck and pulled my torso down. The slam of the cantina owner's knee into my stomach knocked me to my knees. Fucking hell.

The other guy had recovered and grabbed my arm. They yanked me toward the door. I fought their grip with all my might. Never leaving her. Never.

"No. Stop. I *am* with him," Soraya screamed.

They didn't pause or listen to her. We made it to the door and I swung my leg and one guy fell. The other still had an arm.

"Stop. Please. We are friendly. We are friends with Primitivo Borrego de la Cruz," she screeched.

Stillness fell over the room like settling dust after a grenade explosion. All eyes pinned to Soraya.

I used their stunned silence to get to my feet and draw my weapon from my shoulder holster.

The cantina owner pulled a pocket knife and grabbed Soraya around the neck.

Fuck.

He pressed the point to her throat. I tamped back the fury blazing inside me. Losing control would kill us both.

Everyone waited for someone to make a move.

The old man signaled for one of the younger guys to take the knife and Soraya. She looked terrified as they did the switch. The owner dialed on a landline phone beneath the bar. "Cousin, I have a man here who says he knows Primitivo Borrego de la Cruz. Yes. Call Manuel."

Shit. Within seconds all of Tamulipas County would know someone associated with Primitivo Borrego de la Cruz was in this bar. I wished I had asked Falcon more about his history here and why he would tell us to use his name.

"What do you know of Primitivo?" the old man asked me.

"I won't talk before you let her go."

"Talk first."

"I know nothing of him."

"Then you lie." He nodded to the back of the cantina. The man holding Soraya jerked her by her neck and pulled her to a door.

Fucking hell. He just lost his teeth. First chance I got, kicking them into this head.

"Drop your gun." The other man had pulled his gun and turned it on me.

I hesitated. Unarmed we were dead in the water.

"Drop it or we kill her."

I heard a thump and Soraya screamed from the back room. I lowered my weapon to the floor and held up my hands.

Goddamn mother fuckers.

Chapter 16

―――――

"Where is Primitivo?" Two hours after the owner made the phone call, five guys showed up in the back room of the cantina. Not locals there to drink beer in a bar. These were full-on narco gang bangers.

Two of them kids. Under twenty-five. White socks pulled up to their knees. They'd be easier to take out. From the *RC* in their tats, I made out the owner had turned us over to the Reynosa Cartel. They were known for brazen, brutal decapitations in the fight for territory here. Two older men stood behind the chair I'd been bound to. The one who'd asked me the question was the oldest of the five. Maybe thirty-five, forty. He wore a cheap polyester suit, gold chains around his neck, and an oversized Rolex on his wrist. A drug cartel honcho. A buchon. These guys didn't mess around. To survive to his age in a cartel and become a boss, he must be wise and vicious. He and his two guards would be harder to outsmart, but I could do it.

The way he spit Falcon's real name made it obvious Falcon had crossed this dude in a bad way. Fuck Falcon "Primitivo de la Cruz" for sending me into his territory making me an easy target and her a babe in the woods.

The narco boss's right fist pummeled my left cheek. I rocked back in the chair and sucked up the pain. *Strong like bull.* The phrase I always used to keep steady during stress. Bull riding, BUD/S training, beatings from my dad, threats from Greco.

I'd survived the most mentally challenging and physically demanding training in the world. I'd faced terrorists in Iraq and Afghanistan. A narco boss from Tamulipas would not be the one to take me down.

Soraya whimpered from the couch across the room where she was tied at her hands and feet. The original guys from the bar had left and one of the kids held a knife to her throat, but his eyes watched me and the buchon. Good. As long as they kept their attention on me, they'd leave her alone.

"When did you last see Primitivo?" The buchon's accent was sharper, more like Southern Mexico.

I shook my head. "Don't know anyone by that name."

He slugged me in the gut. I grunted and doubled over through the pain. Soraya started to cry. I'd get through this. I just wished like fuck she wasn't watching. I never wanted her to see me like this. Weak.

Strong like bull.

"The rumor is he joined the American military. The fucking traitor. Killed his brother and left the country to fight for the other side."

Yeah. Falcon should've let me in on that little fact before sending us here. "Never heard of him."

"Your bitch over there says you know him."

"She's mistaken."

He withdrew an ice pick from his pocket. His eyes went crazy as he held it in front of my face. Fuck. "Torrez the bull, right? You know what we do to bulls in Tamulipas? We castrate them."

Oh shit.

He stabbed the knife into the crotch of my jeans, the tip thudding on the wooden chair. Soraya screamed. He missed. Probably because my balls were up high right now scared as fuck.

"Quiet!" I gritted through my teeth. She needed to shut up and let me handle this. "I got this under control."

He stabbed me again and this time hit skin. Ow. Fuck. The pain burned from my balls to my neck. Fuck.

Strong like bull.

I needed a distraction. Not Soraya. Something else to get his mind off skewering my balls. If he looked away for a split second, I could reach the blade in my calf holster. I'd still be outnumbered, but I could pull it off.

Soraya started talking. Fast. "I didn't mean it. You know. I uh, I don't know Primitivo. I'm crazy. See?" She swirled her eyes and stuck out her tongue. "If you could just let us go, that would be great."

When they turned to look at her, I snagged my blade from my calf and started working on my rope. The door slammed open, crashing hard and loud against the wall. Three men in black ski masks and full battle gear entered the room with rifles drawn. Please, God. Let them be on my side.

The man taking point shot the narco boss in the back. His eyes widened in shock and his face went flat. Before he dropped, the two other men in the doorway fired on the guards behind me. They grunted and hit the floor, gasping and choking. The kid on the couch got a shot off but missed. He looked terrified. And he should be. I worked the rope off my wrists and ankles and made it to Soraya quickly. I slashed her bindings and landed on top of her to protect her. I didn't see who fired on the last two narcos in the room, but they gasped and gurgled as their lives left them.

"Oh my god. Oh my god." Soraya's fingernails clawed into my shoulders.

"It's okay, babe. It's over now."

I lifted her and carried her over to our point man. The shooter raised his mask. I knew it!

Falcon Primitivo Borrego de la Cruz grinned at me like he'd won the lottery. "Damn that felt good. Been waiting a long time for a chance to kill those fuckers."

The other two men moved quickly, placing their weapons near the hands of the bodies. "Clear out." I recognized Dallas's voice. My best friend. My brother. Saved my ass yet again. The other shooter was most likely Rogan.

Falcon ran out the back door. We all followed him, me carrying Soraya, to a sedan. Falcon took the wheel and Dallas took shotgun. I got in the back with Soraya and the last guy; I didn't know who he was yet. We tore up the dust as we fled the scene.

They all pulled off their face coverings, revealing they were who I thought they were. Falcon, Dallas, and Rogan.

"Too fucking close, you guys. Too fucking close." They let it go much too far.

"She okay?" Rogan inspected Soraya in my lap.

Soraya shivered, curled up, burrowing into my arms. I spoke softly in her ear. The men and I had been through battles like this many times. She was terrified.

"Teimosa. You are safe. You are in my arms and safe. No one will hurt you. Please calm down."

She didn't answer. Her trembles broke into crying. I felt her tears in my gut. I pulled off my shirt and pressed it to the blood on her throat. "Are you hurt anywhere else?"

She shook her head. She'd be okay. We'd made it out. My balls stung and I'd have some bruises, but we'd made it out alive.

"Good, meu amor. That's all that matters. You're not hurt. God, I love you. Thought I'd go insane if they hurt you. If Rogan's team hadn't arrived, I was gonna kill those fuckers myself for putting their hands on you and scaring you. You did great. You were amazing. I'm proud of you."

She sobbed into my chest. "I'm so... sorry." Her shoulders heaved.

"Hush. We'll talk later."

"But I..."

"We'll talk later. Right now. Deep breaths. Calm down. Listen to my heart. Feel my arms around you." I gave her a firm squeeze. She felt so tiny curled up in a ball in my lap. "I love you, Teimosa. I love you."

That seemed to help. She let out a deep breath and her crying ebbed. Within a minute, she'd fallen asleep. A rare, but not unexpected, reaction to trauma. I wasn't worried about her.

Blood stained my pant leg and the pain in my balls reminded me I'd been punctured. "Shit. My balls are bleeding."

Falcon laughed. "We got you out by the skin of your cojones. He was ready to serve up Rocky Mountain oysters."

He found this funny? "*You* set us up, you fucker." I pointed at Falcon in the driver's seat. As soon as we got Soraya safe, I'd have to plant my fist in his face.

He glanced over his shoulder at us. "I had your back the whole time."

"What do you mean?"

"Rogan assigned me to shadow you and her."

I turned my gaze to Rogan who was grinning next to me, holding his rifle, proud of a job well executed.

"I told you I didn't need backup," I said to Rogan.

"You needed us." No hint of regret in his voice. "Dallas asked me to send someone to watch your six. Falcon wanted to do it."

Falcon shrugged. "I like Teimosa. Her dress in Biloxi was hot as fuck."

"Shut the fuck up, Primitivo. If you were in Biloxi, you didn't stop her from getting shot?"

"I thought you had it covered inside the casino. Why do you think they didn't follow you?" Falcon was the reason we weren't followed in Biloxi?

"Did you get some lead into those hitmen? I recognized one as Helix."

"No, I just scared the hell out of them. Watched them race out of the casino. There's no fun in killing them. Then the game would be over."

"This isn't a game, Falcon. Her life is at stake."

He nodded, but he was fucking with me. He loved the game, no matter who died.

"What the hell did you do to that narco boss?" Must've been heinous if they wanted to find him so bad.

His face grew solemn. "He killed a lot of people. Men and women. Now I have removed his stain from my home country."

"You coulda given us more warning. Soraya said your name not knowing she would spark a war."

He shook his head. "I didn't think she'd say my name."

"Well, she did."

"Are they following?" Falcon tried to change the subject.

I checked out the back of the vehicle and didn't see anyone.

"All clear." Rogan confirmed my observation.

"Debrief me, Dallas." So much had gone down, we needed to correlate our stories.

"Falcon called me in when you headed to the border. We clocked Soraya entering the cantina, and we took up position outside. We listened to the phone call and knew trouble was on the way. We went back to the hotel to get more gear. By the time we returned, the buchon had you both in the back room. The rifle we positioned in the kid's hand was marked with the sign of Reynosa's biggest rival, making it look like the kid had turned on the boss."

"Gratitude, brothers. For me. For her. I know I didn't ask for it, but you saved my ass. I owe you huge. Thank you for saving her."

"She clearly means a lot to you," Rogan said.

"She does. That's why I'm going after Greco myself. You guys watch her for me."

Falcon shook his head. "I'll do it for you. Make up for this."

"Nope. Want you on her while I track Greco down."

"Hold up," Dallas interrupted. "Give the hit on Greco a little more time."

"Helix caught up to me once, not risking it again."

"Trust me on this. My best men are on it."

I did trust Dallas. When we served together, he'd saved our necks many times with his intuition and practicality. He had a huge team of Special Forces operators at his disposal. One of them should be able to ice Greco for me and collect the bounty. "Alright. One more week. Let's go pick up the RV at La Real Inn. Not leaving that rig behind unless I'm forced to. We'll split up. Rogan and Dallas go back to Boston. I'm assuming you want to get back to your women?"

"Truth." I locked eyes with Dallas in the rearview mirror. "I left Cyan alone in bed for you."

Rogan nodded. "I never leave Tess longer than absolutely necessary."

So we'd agreed. "Falcon, Soraya, and I will take the RV to my beach house in Galveston."

Falcon swung the car around and headed back to the hotel to get the rig. "See, I told ya you needed me."

Chapter 17

─────

We retrieved the RV and made it through the border without incident. Falcon's maniacal grin had not left his face in the six hours we'd been driving through Texas. He sat in the driver's seat with his hands high on the wheel.

"You take too much joy from the slaughter," I said to him. "Lives were lost. Are you totally immune to it?"

"I've been a sniper and a hitman. You have to be immune. Killing Manuel fulfilled a long-time fantasy of mine."

His fantasies involved murdering five people. Mine involved Soraya naked. "You never should've put Soraya in the crosshairs like you did."

"You took her to Mexico. Not me."

"Your idea." He intentionally sent us in to find trouble. He knew Manuel had a vendetta against him, and he sent us in blind.

"Shoulda known not to trust me."

"Fuck you." Falcon frustrated the hell out of me but for some intangible reason, I still trusted him.

"C'mon, Torrez. If you had a chance to legit wipe out Greco and his top four with no repercussions, you wouldn't send a woman in with me as a decoy?"

I understood where he was coming from, but not with my girl. "I might, but I'd let you in on the plan before I sent you."

"You had to know." He gave me a side-eye raised brow.

"I had a feeling. But no idea how fucking insane you are."

He threw his head back and laughed. "Totally. Now you're completely aware. Any further missions between us, you must admit you have been informed of my loco-ness."

I headed to the back to check on Soraya. My weight tipping the side of the bed woke her up. She blinked away sleep and propped up on her elbows. She looked out the bedroom door to the empty eating area. "Where is everyone?"

"Rogan and Dallas flew back to Boston." I pressed her shoulder to encourage her to lay back down.

She pushed up in the bed and leaned against the wall. "Who's driving?"

"Falcon. He's coming with us to my beach house in Galveston."

She swiped her hair from her face. Her mouth turned down. "Torrez. I'm sorry. I was stupid. I created so much trouble."

"It's okay."

"It's not okay. I betrayed you." She covered her eyes with her hands. "Can you ever forgive me?" She peeked through a space she made by opening her palms.

"Is that what you want? My forgiveness?" She lowered her arms and I caught her gaze. "Because you chose to leave." I kept my voice soft, but the pain her betrayal caused me rang loud and clear.

"That was a huge mistake."

"You told them you weren't with me." She shook her head slowly. "If you want out, you don't need my forgiveness. You're free to go."

"Please, don't." She lowered her head and rested it in her palm.

"If you believe I'm the bad guy keeping you against your will, you're free to go. I won't hold you back anymore."

Her sweet worried eyes peered up at me. "I don't want to leave you."

"And I should believe you now?"

"Yes. I was scared. I panicked and ran." She placed a delicate hand on my thigh. I wanted to kiss her fingertips, her neck, her breast. Kiss away all the pain I'd caused her. "It wasn't rational," she continued. "Everything I did and said was stupid. I let my fears rule, and I almost got us both killed."

"You did."

"When I saw them hurt you, I died inside. I couldn't stand it. If they killed you, I would've asked them to kill me too. A strong, fierce, undeniable force took over my heart. Love..."

Staring into her beautiful eyes, I asked her, "Love?"

She nodded. "More sure than life itself. I felt it for you before, but I doubted it. I didn't believe I could be loved, but I saw in your fight how much you loved me and I believe it now."

Shit, if going through hell made her realize she loved me, then I'd do it over again and beg Manuel to spear my balls with an ice pick.

"I do, Teimosa. Glad you finally see it."

"I'm so sorry." She sounded tortured and sincere.

"Loyalty is important to me." She needed to get that if she was gonna love me. "You'll have to trust me one hundred percent." I leaned in close and held her cheek in my palm.

She tilted her head into my hand. Her big brown eyes looked so vulnerable and childlike. "I do. I promise. If you can forgive me, we can make it through anything. We're super powerful together."

"I can forgive you." My thumb caressed her skin. "It's forgotten."

She smiled.

"We need time," I said. "We both need to heal." This would all pass and we could pick up where we left off.

"Okay."

Bringing my lips close to hers, I pinned her with my eyes. She held her breath, waiting for what I would say. "But as soon as possible, I'm fucking your ass."

"Oh my god." Her mouth dropped open in a shocked *O*.

"We get to my beach house, you heal. We'll get rid of Falcon because I don't want him listening in. Then I'll fuck your ass. You'll be mine. You can't leave me after I've claimed your ass."

A shy smile grew on her sweet lips. "That's ridiculous."

"Is it? You'll see. Once you've felt me inside you like no one has ever been before, our souls will be bonded forever."

"Will it hurt?"

"A little. But you'll like it."

She shivered and bit her lip.

"I'm not leaving!" Falcon's voice from the driver's seat penetrated our bubble in the little bed.

"Fuck you!" I yelled back.

"I'm staying to watch you fuck her ass. Now that's something I need to see." He kept talking to himself in Spanish, going over the details of what he would see.

I slammed the thin door and locked it. He would never see shit. I'd never let anyone see Soraya naked and definitely didn't want an audience when we did it that way for the first time.

Chapter 18

––––––––

I helped her back down to the bed and curled in behind her. The RV rocked and the engine hummed. She lay quiet for a long time, but didn't sleep. The warmth of healing floated between our bodies. I'd forgive her and we'd be closer than ever before.

"A beach house in Galveston?" she asked.

"Yep. It's amazing. Right on the ocean. Private boardwalk to the sand." One of my favorite houses of all I had built over the years.

"Will I meet your kids?"

Her mentioning them tugged at the empty space in my heart when I was away from them. "Hope so. I want you to meet them. I've got video surveillance set up on them. But still want to be close in case Greco has figured out their location."

"Will I meet your ex-wife?" she asked a little more quietly.

"Unfortunately, yes. Jacqueline comes with the kids. I'll try to minimize your exposure to her."

She turned around and looked in my eyes. "It's okay. I'm curious to see the woman stupid enough to let you go."

"She didn't. I left her. I tried to stay for my kids, but a man can only stand by watching his wife cheat for so long before his own needs take over."

"What do you mean?"

"I stayed faithful."

"You did?"

"The last time I had sex with Jacqueline was when Peyton was conceived."

"Wow. You sacrificed so much for them."

"I had to. They needed me to look out for them. Ironic part is as soon as I left, she changed her tune. Stopped sleeping with Greco. Wanted me back. Even after years of telling me I was shit. The second I left, she started begging."

"But you never went back?"

"No. Damage was done. Talked it over with my kids. Made it clear I wasn't leaving them, just her. Anything they needed, they could ask me. She didn't treat them right, they let me know."

"And did she treat them right?"

"Surprisingly, she's a good mom. I made sure she spent the money on them first before she got any spending cash. Kept her in line. Now she's remarried, she's his problem. Kids are older, I send the money direct to them."

"What's her new husband like?"

"Puny. White. Salesman. Safe. She had enough adventure I guess and went the opposite route. You can still do that, you know? Find yourself a man who won't have my history and the risks that come with being with me."

"No, never. I don't want anybody else. I want you no matter the risks. I love you." She said it again. Felt just as good to hear as the first time.

"Love you too, babe. So much. I'll make it good for us. You'll feel safe. I promise."

"I don't need safe. I like life on the road. It's fun."

I laughed. "We'll have other kinds of fun. After you're healed." I peeled the bandage back on her neck and checked the wound. Bleeding stopped. "This one will heal faster than the one on your breast. A slice heals faster than a tear." I kissed the skin of her neck next to her bandage. "I'm sorry, Teimosa. I'm sorry you were hurt." If the blade had gone half an inch deeper, she'd be dead.

Her hands wrapped behind my neck and rubbed my scalp. "It's okay. I'm fine. How are you?" She pulled away and looked down at my pants. "Did they hurt your balls?"

"A bit of blood. Amazing how a tiny cut in that spot can hurt so bad. But it'll heal. I'll still be able to have kids." Her eyes popped wide open. "Do you want kids?"

"I... I don't know. I didn't with Yegor. I took birth control without him knowing. I was going to pretend to be infertile to avoid having children with him."

"It's been a long time for me, but if you wanted it, I'd love to have kids with you. They'd be so beautiful if they looked like you."

Her head fell back and she sighed. "It's nice to think about. I've always dreamed of being a mom. I've never seriously thought it would happen."

"Start thinking. Anything you want can happen now. Make a list of your all-time most unattainable dreams and prepare for them to come true."

"Okay." She snuggled deeper into my arms. It felt good. "And what do you dream of, Torrez?"

I kissed the top of her head and thought about it. It had been a vague picture before now. But driving out to my beach house, with her in my arms, talking about my kids, it all came into focus. "I dream of holding you like this forever. Want you in my kitchen, singing bad rap songs in your red pajamas. Want to take you out and show you off in your sexy dresses. Want my kids close by and you by my side every day." I turned her to face me. Her eyes glistened. I was getting through to her, and my plan was coming to life with my words. "I wanna take you to Kemah Boardwalk with the kids. Ride the roller coaster. Eat funnel cakes and laugh in the summer air. Most of all, I want you sleeping next to me every night. Listening to the ocean. Watching the seasons change. Want to wake up and your face is the first thing I see, your tits, the second, and want your sweet pussy to be my breakfast every morning."

Her cheeks turned red and her faced curled into an ugly cry as the first drop escaped her eyes. But Soraya was never ugly. Her ugly cry was adorable, just like everything about her. "You want to be a lawyer, I'll drive you to law school and back every day. I'll deliver your resume to all the top firms till you have the perfect dream job. You want to be a model, we need to talk because I don't trust that dude who offered you a modeling contract. But I check him out, make sure he's legit, you can be a model in Paris if you like. I'll be sitting in the front row at every show. Grinning like a fool because that's my girl up there."

That was it for her. She dropped her forehead to my chest, gripped my biceps, and sobbed. "What is it, babe? No one's ever cared about your happiness before? Those days are over. Our lives revolve around your fulfillment. Because if my girl is happy, I'm happy too."

"Oh, Torrez, that's so beautiful." The wistfulness in her voice told me she still didn't believe it could happen for us.

"It's within our reach. Don't tell yourself it's not."

"I want to make you happy too." Her head popped up and I smiled into her red eyes. "You've had so much negative in your life. From your dad, to your ex-wife, to Greco. All of them beating you down, telling you you're shit. Have you ever had a positive, healthy relationship where the woman cared about you and respected you?"

I shook my head. "No."

"Why?"

"Good question. Easy answer is I was focused on work and the kids and didn't want to bring anyone into this mess. Harder answer is I didn't trust anyone to get close and never let a woman in."

"Didn't anyone try? I can't imagine a man like you walking around Siege doesn't get a lot of attention."

"You know about Siege?" The backdoor activities at Siege were top secret except for the folks who chose to participate.

"Know what? I know it's a nightclub and there's lots of hot commandos and girls looking to snag one. Is there more to it than that?"

"Yes, but I can't tell you about it, and it doesn't matter to you. There were women at Siege who wanted to get close to me. I kept them at a distance."

"But you let me in?"

"You jackhammered your way in. Blasted through all my defenses the first night."

"Good. I'll be the one then. The one to tell you over and again how tremendously awesome you are. You need to hear it because you've gone too long without it. You've earned my respect and love."

I kissed her and she smiled. "We could be so good together, Teimosa." I spoke against the tears wetting her lips.

"Yes."

"Rest now. Heal. When you wake up, the world will be yours."

"Okay. Will you stay?"

"I will stay. Never leaving you. I will stay."

Chapter 19

Soraya

Torrez squeezed my hand and rang the bell of a giant estate home in La Marque, Texas. Arriving at dinnertime made me nervous. I didn't want to interrupt them if they were eating. I adjusted the buttons of my blouse to line up a bit straighter, cover more boob. Darn, I should've dressed more conservatively to meet Torrez' family. Oh well, skinny jeans and red sparkles is who I am, so they'd be getting the real me.

"They're fake." Torrez glanced at my cleavage.

"No they aren't." I let go of his hand and tucked my hair behind my ears. "Don't piss me off right now. I'm already nervous."

"Not yours. Hers." He tipped his head toward the front door.

"Oh..."

I masked my surprised laugh as a skinny blonde woman opened the door. Her eyes bugged out and scanned me from head to toe and up again, narrowing when she saw his arm leading behind my back. Being scrutinized by this stranger with a long history with Torrez rattled my already frayed nerves. Too bad Falcon wasn't here for moral support, but he'd left for town saying he didn't do ex-wives or kids.

"Soraya, this is Jacqueline." After Torrez motioned from me to her, the warmth from his palm returned to my spine like a comforting hug.

"Jackie." She corrected Torrez with frustration in her tone as she tilted her head and offered me a stiff smile. Both her hands clasped my one right hand. The oversized ring on her left finger flopped to the side, like a lollipop ring with a huge jewel-shaped candy.

Torrez was right. Jackie had looks traditionally considered beautiful, especially in America. Tall thin frame, long platinum hair, sleepy princess eyes, tan skin, white teeth.

An oversized leather belt cinched her shirt around her miniscule waist. Her tight top and leggings had a Peg Bundy feel to them. Her nails were done in baby blue to match her shirt and her square earrings. Her white platform pumps matched her belt and her pants. I kinda liked her style. It was unique and bold, not afraid to let it show she took care of herself. A twinge of jealousy ran down my spine. Her boobs looked sexy, and she was thinner than I'd ever be.

The gentle touch of Torrez' fingertip traced my arm from my elbow to my shoulder. *They're not real*. Ahh. That helped. Torrez had made it abundantly clear he loved my curves. Jackie was all pointy bones and sharp edges.

I straightened my spine and gave her a confident smile. "Pleasure to meet you, Jackie."

"Come in." She pursed her lips and stared at Torrez' backside as we walked past. She made an appreciative "mmm-mmm" sound.

Holy crap. She still checks him out? You know what, biatch? He's not yours anymore. He's all mine.

Just to piss her off I patted Torrez three times on the most tantalizing part of his ass, the round of his left butt cheek. The part I can touch whenever I like.

Screw her. Eat your heart out, Jackie.

As if he sensed the tension between us, Torrez adjusted the position of his gun in his hip holster. His T-shirt hung over his jeans enough to hide the fact he was carrying a gun, but he made that gesture for Jackie's benefit.

Jackie finished inspecting his body, and her gaze landed on his face. "Still getting in brawls, I see." Jackie nodded at the blue and purple bruise forming around Torrez' left eye.

He ignored her and his arm moved up around my shoulder to guide me from the foyer into the living room.

Whoa. Jackie's "ranch house" looked more like a rustic French chateau. Thick creamy drapes adorned the windows. Lavish couches shined like pearls. Marble tile led to a grand staircase made of wrought iron and stressed timber. It twisted up and off to either side where a balcony on the second floor looked down on the open living room. The contrast of the black iron against all the white took my breath away.

Torrez smiled as I gawked at the staircase and balcony. "Did you build this?"

He lowered his arm from around my shoulders and beamed with pride. "I did. You like?"

"It's exquisite."

"Yes." Jackie sounded unimpressed with her refined mansion that I knew Torrez had broken his back to build for her and his kids. "Shame we have to sell it."

"Why do you need to sell it?" Torrez sounded impatient with her already.

"We can't afford it."

"It's paid for."

"Yes, but the air conditioning alone is enough to break our bank."

"Your man can't even pay to heat and cool this place?"

"Duffy works on commission. The pool industry is slowing down." She stepped close to him and put her hands on his biceps. "It's so stressful. Worrying about money. Losing the house. The kids..." She peered up at him with puppy-dog eyes. He held her at a distance. He wasn't embracing her but still the contact between them made my blood boil. She shouldn't have touched him like that. They were not married and he was with me. She tilted her neck in an awkward attempt to rest her forehead on his chest. She was making a play for him right in front of me. Little witch.

Torrez pushed her back by her shoulders, and his face turned to a dark scowl. "Cut the shit, Jacqueline." He released her with a small push. "Duffy can't sell a pool in Texas, he needs to find another gig."

She glared at him with indignant shock. What did she expect? He'd hug you and give you money? Not likely. This was a show for my benefit. She was trying to make it seem like they had that kind of relationship, but I believed Torrez when he said he hadn't slept with her since Peyton was conceived.

"Mmm. Interesting coming from you, Torrez. Duffy doesn't give up. *He* sticks with his commitments through tough times."

"Where're the kids?" He kept his voice even but sharp.

"At least you've stuck with *Greco*, right?" She used Greco's name like a weapon, her sword against the blade he had drawn with his voice. She turned her gaze to mine and said with intention, "Torrez is in the Mafia, you know?" Torrez flexed his fingers over his gun like he was doing everything he could not to pull it out and shoot her. "He's one of them. A gangster. A kingpin. Be careful with—"

"Lies. And you know it. I'm not in the Mafia. I wouldn't even be affiliated with Greco if you weren't fucking him and bleeding cash so fast, he was the only option to dig me and my kids out of the pit of hell *you* created. My association with Greco paid for this house, that kitchen," he pointed to a doorway through which I could see a chef's kitchen decorated in the same classy style as the rest of the house, "even though you got no idea how to use it."

She rolled her eyes and kept talking to me. "He's not an honorable man."

Oh that was it. She couldn't talk about my man like that, saying the words I knew would trigger him. "He's the most honorable man I know. He saved me many times over, sacrificing himself for my freedom. Just as he did for all his years of service in the military. If you think he's not honorable, you need to get yourself a dictionary and look up the meaning of the word because you'll see his face there. He took an ice pick in his balls for me!"

Torrez sputtered and smiled at me. "Thank you, babe." He turned a scowl back on Jacqueline. "And I'm here to inform you, *Jackie*, I'm out. It's over. I'm done with Greco forever. So tell your man to start selling some pools. As soon as the kids are out of your house, you'll never see another dime from me."

While he was talking, Jackie's mouth slowly dropped open, preparing to say something but only uttering a few grunts. "I—"

"And that could be as soon as tomorrow. We're moving into my beach house and the kids are welcome to stay full-time."

We were moving into his beach house? I hadn't even seen it yet, but the way he described it sounded amazing. Kids? Full-time?

"I have custody." Jackie crossed her arms under her boobs and finally formed a response.

"You have partial custody, and they're old enough to make up their own minds."

She grunted some more and flapped her jaw like a Koi fish.

"Now. Where're the kids?" Torrez disregarded her and looked around the house.

"Oh, they should be home soon."

"I told you what time we'd arrive."

"Yes, well, you know teenagers."

I wouldn't be surprised if she hadn't told the kids a later time so she could have her chance to get her digs into Torrez' back. I also guessed Torrez would have told his kids what time to meet us.

A squeaking on the tile in the hallway revealed a tall, handsome young man with green eyes and curly dark hair bounding into the room as he tucked his car keys in his pocket. His smile grew into a replica of Torrez' and he hugged his father. "Hey, Dad."

"Good to see you, Drew. Missed you."

"Missed you too."

Behind Drew trailed a shorter girl with lighter hair and brown eyes. Still beautiful, but she definitely resembled her mother more than Torrez.

"My Peyton." Torrez' face lit up as he held his arms wide for her.

She ran the last few steps and slammed her head into his chest. "Daddy."

He wrapped his arms around her, closed his eyes, and pressed a tender kiss to the top of her head. No matter the truth about paternity, she was his girl.

The love between father and children flowed like a visceral river through the huge room. Jackie stood stiffly as she watched the effusive family reunion. I swallowed the thickness in my throat. No one in my life, except Torrez, had hugged me like that. And I'd never hugged a child before. I'd spent very little time around children in my isolated life in the palace and boarding schools.

"This is my girlfriend, Soraya." Torrez pressed his hand to my back and moved to the side.

His what? I guess I was his girlfriend. I just hadn't thought of it in such official terms before.

Drew stepped in and gave me a hug that warmed me to my bones. Oh my god. I'd been missing out on children and hugs like this? If I'd known what I was missing, I'd have been even more miserable. I gripped Drew's shoulders and sniffled through an awkward laugh. Drew released me and stepped back.

"Soraya, this is my girl, Peyton." The pride in Torrez' voice, the hesitance in her eyes. Too much. Too much. If Peyton hugged me, the tears would flow. I couldn't embrace an adorable girl like her without balling like a baby.

I bent my knees and smiled at her with my arms slowly opening.

Her lips quirked and her head tilted to the side as she stepped in and gave me the sweetest hug of all time. Yes, the tears dropped. I spoke softly in her ear. "You're lovely. Thank you for the hug. I'm so happy to meet you."

We separated and looked around. Jackie's hard stare had softened. Torrez' eyes glowed with love and adoration.

He slung one arm around my shoulder and one around Peyton's. "We're going to Kemah Boardwalk. I'll have them back by..."

"What do we have here?" A man entered the room from the hallway and kept his eyes on Torrez as he stopped next to Jackie. A pleasant looking man. Slim, with thinning brown hair. He wore khaki slacks and a striped blue and white button-down shirt. Nothing exciting like my Torrez and his camo pants and black tees that looked like they were made to be worn by him.

"Duffy." Torrez kept his voice respectful.

Jackie had to bend down to kiss Duffy on the cheek. Duffy's eyes glanced in Jackie's direction as if that were enough to greet her.

"This is my girlfriend, Soraya." Torrez spoke in a deep authoritative tone. "We're taking the kids out for the night. We'll have them back at eleven."

"Alright then." Duffy tried to make it sound like he had a say in the matter when it was clear he didn't.

"You kids ready?" Torrez asked them with fun in his voice.

"Yes!"

"How'd you like to ride in a bigass RV?"

"Torrez," Jackie scolded him.

"Excuse me. How'd you like to ride in an RV that is pimped out as fuck?"

"Yes!" Peyton jumped on her toes and Drew grinned at Torrez. Oh yes, they adored their dad, they didn't mind him cursing, and they loved the goodies he brought home for them.

"Let's go." Torrez didn't say goodbye to Jackie and Duffy, but I waved to them as we turned and walked out the front door.

Chapter 20

‍———‍

"Night, Peyton." I hugged Peyton as we stood together inside the door to the RV. It was ten minutes before eleven, so they would be home exactly on time.

"Night, Soraya. I had so much fun." Peyton smiled at me and glanced at her dad. "I'm glad my dad found you. You make him happier than I've ever seen him."

"Really?"

"My dad, he hides it good, but I can tell he's lonely. He's never brought a girlfriend home before, but he looks at you like you could light the moon."

"Aww, thank you so much. Your dad makes me happy too."

"Yay!" She clapped her hands.

I had noticed Torrez' perma-grin as I ate my first funnel cake—which was delicious—and rode my first roller coaster—which was terrifying. I'd attributed his joy to being with his kids, but it was nice to think I contributed to his contented demeanor.

"Will you be here tomorrow?" Peyton grabbed the giant stuffed bucking bronco Torrez had won for her at the shooting gallery.

My gaze flitted to Torrez in the front seat where he was saying goodnight to Drew. Torrez nodded.

"Yes. I'll be here tomorrow. Hopefully I'll be here a lot."

"Awesome! Bye."

She burst out the door of the RV and ran up the long drive of the ranch house. Drew followed behind her. "Later, Raya." Drew had given me the nickname as the night started out. He'd tried to act like he didn't like kid stuff, but he'd smiled and had a blast all night.

Torrez checked his phone as the kids reached the door. "Fucking shit!"

"What?"

"Nothing."

"It's something. Let me see."

He held up the screen. An app showed a live camera image of the inside of Jackie's house. I jutted my finger out and hit the button to un-mute it.

Jackie's grumbling slurs filled the cab of the RV. "Damn Torrez and his shiny new toy." Jackie stumbled up the grand staircase, Duffy trying to hold her up—by her ass—while her back rubbed on the wall.

"Jackie, baby. Let's get you to bed." Duffy pulled up on her butt, and her arms flopped over his shoulders. He grunted as he tried to lift her, but her body slouched like dead weight, and he only raised her one inch before she fell back into her position against the wall.

"I was his new toy once," she slurred.

"Can we stop talking about this?" Duffy replied.

"She's big and curvy. Do men even like that?"

He hesitated. "Most men like curves."

She stared up at him with her mouth open, her eyes drawn. "I had two men. Greco couldn't get enough of me. Maybe Torrez wanted me to be rounder."

"Okay. That's it. I was gonna try to fuck you, but now my dick is totally soft with you going on about your exes. Walk your skinny ass up these stairs and sleep it off." He slung an arm around her waist and tugged her side up against his in an awkward dance.

"Oh my." A giggle escaped my throat.

"Don't worry," Torrez said.

"I'm not," I replied. "I'm sure he'll get her to bed eventually."

"No. You never need to worry. If you're drunk, I'm taking you to our room and fucking you. No dicking around on the stairs. Unless, you're too drunk, then I won't fuck you, but either way, you got a man you can rely on to carry you to bed."

The giggle grew to a full-on belly laugh. "That's certainly comforting. What girl doesn't want to be carried to bed when she's drunk?"

He was serious at first, but my laughter drew a chuckle out of him.

"I mean we all have needs, right?" I said, teasing him. "Food, water, get carried to bed drunk..."

His smile spread across his beautiful face and I memorized it. He'd been happier tonight than I'd ever seen him.

I was still snickering when Torrez' shoulders got tight, all his attention zeroed in on his phone, and a glacial ice hit the space between us. After several frantic taps on his phone and some zooming, he muttered, "Fuck."

"What is it?"

He tossed me the phone and raced to the closet by the kitchen area. "Speed dial Jackie. Tell her there's an intruder." Oh no. An intruder? "Looks like Helix. The bounty hunter. West side of the house. Tell her to get the kids to the safe room ASAP." He spoke quickly, an experienced Navy SEAL in charge in an emergency in seconds. I fumbled to get the security app on his phone closed and searched for the phone feature. "No. Fuck!"

"What?" My head snapped up and we locked eyes.

He had gone into fight or flight mode, and my Torrez was preparing to fight. He slipped a bulletproof vest over his head and tightened it with quick ease. "Call Drew first. Tell him to get Peyton to the safe room and buckle down."

"Call Drew first?"

"Yes! Call him now! This is it. I'm taking down Helix. It ends now. Don't panic. God, whatever the fuck you do, do not panic." As he spoke he moved to the door of the RV. I found Drew's number in his priority contacts and hit his call button. "Watch on the phone," Torrez told me. "But stay here. Let me handle this. Do not come after me, understand?"

I wanted to ask more questions, but Torrez had asked me to act quickly if something like this happened. I just nodded and he left.

"Hey, Dad. What's up?" Drew answered my call.

"Drew. Get Peyton to the safe room now. There's an intruder on the west side of the house. Your dad's coming. Hurry!"

He didn't answer but I heard fast footsteps and his voice calling, "C'mon!"

Peyton grunted and I heard a door close.

Drew came back on the line, panting heavily. "She's safe."

"He wants you in there too. He said buckle down."

"Where's my dad?"

"Drew. He told me to stay put and let him handle it. You should do the same."

"No." I heard a door creak open and his breath hitch. "I have my gun."

"Oh no. No. Just hide and wait for him."

"Lavontes don't run. We face the bull by the horns. If you're going to be part of this family, you'd best accept that now."

"Uh. Um." Part of the Lavonte family? The terror in my gut mixed with the warmth of love, which ratcheted up the tension. I finally had a family. I couldn't lose them now!

"Where's my mom?" His breath came through the phone like he was running.

I switched over to the video monitor. Duffy and Jackie had left the stairs.

"I think she's in her room with Duffy."

"Good."

"I found my dad." The phone flashed. A red button on the screen told me the call had been disconnected.

I held my breath and watched on the security app as Torrez and Drew approached a man standing in the kitchen. They both had guns drawn and the intruder was heading straight toward Drew. Holy cow. If they got hurt...

I could run. I could run to him and help.

No. He told me to stay put.

So I hunkered down with my phone lifeline and watched my man and his son face down a man who was there to kill him. But first I had one call to make.

"Falcon."

"Yes, Teimosa? You lonely?"

"The bounty hunter is at Jackie's ranch. Torrez and Drew have him cornered in the kitchen."

"I'm five minutes out."

Chapter 21

---

*T*orrez

No sign of Helix at the kitchen door where I'd seen him. My stomach sank at the thought of him inside the house.

I found him in the kitchen, slithering in the dark along the counter toward the doorway that led to the living room.

"Helix. Over here," I whispered.

Too smart to fall for it, he hit the ground and got a shot off in my direction. Miss.

"Stop!" Drew's voice came from the other side of the kitchen. Chancing a glance around the corner, my heart leapt into my throat at the sight of my son pointing a gun at a lethal bounty hunter, who was pointing his weapon at me.

"Drew. Back off," I warned.

"No, Dad."

Fucking Drew. Eager to be the hero but nowhere near old enough yet.

Helix glanced between us, assessing the risk. He made his decision and switched his aim to Drew. Fuck no. This was not going down that way.

"Helix!" He didn't look at me. "You want me, right? Here I am."
I placed my weapon next to my feet, spread my arms wide, and
walked into the kitchen.

Drew's barrel shook but he held Helix's gaze. His game face was
spot on. He got that from riding the bulls. You show a hint of
fear, the crowd will catch it, the bull will smell it, and you're a
loser before you're out of the gate.

"I got him, I got you," Helix said stupidly, yet totally accurately.
"He's your son, right?"

"Let's take this outside." I wanted any chance to get that barrel
pointed away from Drew.

"He's your son. You'll give up yourself for him." Helix stared at
Drew.

"Absolutely."

Darkness flashed through Helix's eyes. A muscle in his neck
twitched. I found it. His weakness.

"A father gives his life for his son, no question," I said, trying to
touch the human part of him.

He glanced at me for the first time and must have seen the ve-
racity in my face.

"Your dad willing to do that for you? Or is your dad a prick?"

"He doesn't exist."

"I'll take that as your dad's a prick. You can see I'm his world, so you kill me, you kill all three of us here."

He lowered his head.

"Let's go outside. You're here for the money, right?"

Helix raised his head. "Of course. Two mil for you dead? Highest pot I've seen in a long time."

"You check the web lately? That hit's been called off."

"Called off? You're full of shit."

"It's true." Falcon's voice joined the room as he stepped up behind Drew and aimed his weapon at Helix's chest. Drew's eyes widened as he took in the much bigger guy behind him. "Hit on Lavonte is null." The hit hadn't been called off but Falcon played along.

"This place is packed with cameras." I tilted my head to the camera in the corner. "You kill any one of us, you're going down. The cops are on their way. Least you'll get is breaking and entering with a weapon. Felony. You don't have any other strikes do you, Helix?"

"Fuck." He got to his feet and bounced on his toes as his gaze flitted to the two exits. He'd have to go through Falcon and Drew or me.

"Got more news for you, Helix. The hit on Greco is up to ten mil." I lied.

"It is? Who ordered that hit?"

"Don't know. Just know it's still active and he's an easy target. No cameras, no scared as fuck sons pointing weapons at your face, no snipers standing behind him on his side." I nodded at Drew and Falcon. "I'll make you a deal. You run right now. None of us will shoot you in the back. You're free to go. I destroy the video of the breaking and entering. You go after the ten mil and take care of Greco."

I could almost see the gears tattooed on his head turning as he tried to judge my truthfulness. I raised one hand. "Code of honor, man. I'll let you run. This is forgotten. You get Greco."

"What code of honor?"

"Navy."

"I ain't Navy. The syndicate has a much more fucked up code. A code where we'd all be dead by now."

"My code is better. Hand me the weapon. I'll move aside. You can leave. The end." I held my palm flat.

He looked at his weapon, then at me, then at Drew again. His brow creased with pain. Oh yeah, Drew got to him. "Leave me and my boy be. C'mon. Take it or the offer expires and I let my son have his first kill."

Drew's eyebrows shot up, and he locked eyes with me. I nodded slightly to let him know I was in control.

Helix let out a huge sigh. Placed the butt of his weapon in my hand, and kept his eyes locked to mine as he stepped by me. I moved aside and let him pass, keeping his weapon pointed at the floor.

He flew out the back door like a bat out of hell.

Falcon and Drew exhaled and lowered their weapons.

"Holy shit, Dad. That was awesome!"

I'd seen that spark in a man's eye after his first hint of action. "Don't get any ideas, son. It doesn't always end like that."

Falcon laughed. "Usually it ends bloodier. Then it's even more fun."

"Shut up, Primitivo. Go follow him off the property. Clear the rest of the house." Falcon nodded and followed Helix out.

"Come here, boy." Drew walked to me and collapsed in my arms. His shoulders heaved—the bravado gone, the shock working its way in. "I got you. You did so well. Kept your cool under pressure."

He pulled away. His pupils were dilated and his hands shook. "God, Dad. When you walked in with your arms wide, I wanted to pull the trigger then. I wanted to kill him before he could kill you."

"I know. That's always the hardest part. But you did well. You can't get a bullet back in the chamber once it's out. Best to wait and see if you need it. Many times your intellect is the most powerful weapon." I breathed a sigh of relief Drew didn't need to see me kill someone. It would have been just because the guy had a weapon pulled on him, but I was glad my son wouldn't have that memory of me. I wanted him to see me as clean. His hero. Not a man able to shoot someone without conscience.

"Looking back on it, I'm glad I didn't shoot Helix. He's a man like anyone else. He has a family. He may look like a machine, and he's caused me a lot of trouble over the years, so I did want to get even with him, but I got through to him by showing him my love for you. He saw my humanness, and I saw his. We couldn't kill each other over money or some stupid reason."

"Is he going after Greco for you?" Drew asked.

Oh shit. He heard all that. "Listen, Drew. Before anyone comes back into this room. You must never mention Greco or Helix to your mom, Duffy, Peyton, or anyone. You saw some high-level confidential activity tonight, but keeping quiet about it will save your life and all of theirs."

He nodded.

"I'll tell you the truth. Greco is a bad dude. A criminal. And as of right now, he is out to get me. And yes, I believe Helix will take care of him. You never heard of him, hear me?"

"Yes, Dad."

"Thank you."

Jackie and Duffy raced into the room. Jackie rushed to Drew and embraced him. "Are you alright?" She held his head between her hands and inspected his face and body. "Were you hurt? We heard gunshots."

"I'm fine, Mom. There was only one gunshot."

I chuckled because it was true. All that action and only one shot fired. No injuries.

"What happened." Duffy looked at me to explain.

Drew pulled out of his mother's hold and started yapping. "Dad was so awesome. A, uh, burglar, broke in. He was uh, trying to steal stuff."

Jackie looked from him to me to corroborate. I nodded because it worked, and I had no idea Drew possessed advanced lying skills. I'd have to keep a closer eye on him.

Drew continued. "Dad fired a warning shot and he took off running."

"Oh my goodness. Should we call the police?" Jackie asked.

"No, I think he was scared enough," I replied. "Drew, go get Peyton from the safe room."

"Oh thank God Peyton is safe." Jackie put her arms around Duffy.

"Drew got her in there quick." I held up a finger. "One second, I need to check on Soraya."

I called her up on my other phone. "Babe."

"Oh my god, Torrez. I was so worried. I saw the whole thing."

"I'm coming to get you."

"I'm at the front door. Let me in."

I ran to the door and opened it. She jumped into my arms. "Never leave me again. I was so scared."

"You did great. You stayed calm. Got Peyton to safety."

"Drew wouldn't listen to me. I told him to stay in the safe room."

"I know. It all worked out."

She kissed me and crawled up my body. Her tongue plunged into my mouth, desperate to connect. I didn't hesitate and kissed her back, walking to the wall to nail her to it. Her back hit the wall and she gasped. "You're here. I'm okay. Feel me. Here." The adrenaline coursing through us made it all so intense. If all these people weren't in the house...

"A little post action fuck show?" Falcon strolled in through the front door.

"Shut up, Primitivo," Soraya said to him.

I set her down and tucked her under my arm as Falcon approached.

"I chased him to a car and he took off." Falcon wiped his arm across his forehead to clear the sweat.

"Good. Can you get to the security room and delete the footage?"

"You sure we can trust Helix? We might need it to hold against him."

"I think he's good for it."

"Okay. And the hits," he asked low, under his breath.

"Get to the computer in the RV, start a rumor the hit on me was pulled. Change my bid to ten mil."

Drew and Peyton emerged from the hallway. Peyton looked confused but not scared. "What happened, Daddy?"

"There was a burglar. He's gone now. You're safe." I hugged my girl and she hugged me back.

"I know that. You're here. I'm safe."

"Let's go in the kitchen and see if your mom has the ingredients for a pizookie."

"What's a pizookie," Soraya asked.

"You've never had a pizookie?" Peyton seemed shocked. "It's only the best cookie ice cream sundae ever and my dad makes the best ones. We have the ingredients. I make sure to add them to the shopping list every week."

"Sounds good. Let's go." I wrapped my arm over Soraya's shoulder and guided her to the kitchen.

———

A WEEK AFTER THE INCIDENT at Jackie's place, I got a text on my burner phone from DNA, Helix's code name. He sent a picture. Greco. Almost unrecognizable with a least five shots to the face.

DNA: Pay up.

I didn't respond, but I knew he'd be happy when ten million bucks appeared in his account.

I called Falcon on a burner phone.

"Esta muerto." *He's dead.* I didn't need to say Greco's name. Falc knew a ten mil hit would go fast.

"Excellente," he replied. "You get me now? It's satisfying, right? Knowing he's gone from this earth?"

"I get you. Still wouldn't drag your woman into danger, but I get you."

"I ain't got a woman. Problem solved."

"You need a woman."

"Absolutely do not."

"Alright. I need a favor."

He laughed. "You already owe me a few."

"I do, but this one is the most important. Watch over Soraya for me. About a week."

"You trust me with her?"

"You've become a friend, Falc."

He grunted.

"Come to Galveston. Beaches are sweet."

"You going after her ex?"

Falcon's thoughts went straight there. "Can't say." But yes, most definitely was going after him myself.

"You need a man?" he asked.

"No, and you'd better not shadow me. Need you on her while I'm gone."

He remained quiet for a moment. "Be there Monday."

"Excellente."

Chapter 22

Soraya

After Torrez returned from his mystery trip, we spent the most glorious six weeks of my life at his beach house in Galveston. He'd built a gorgeous mansion out on the south side of the island. An aged wooden boardwalk took us to our own little stretch of beach on the Gulf.

Long stilts lifted the house above sea level. Four stories, each with a full wrap-around balcony. Inside, friendly chocolate and teal decor made the house much more earthy and lived in than Jackie's stuffy chateau. The sound of the ocean played in every room, and the sun greeted us in the mornings through huge scalloped bay windows. We spent our days walking along the shore or reading out on one of the three decks. Just being there relaxed me. All our cares seemed to blow away on the wind.

In the evenings, Torrez cooked tasty traditional Brazilian specialties for me. My favorite was coxinhas. Fried croquettes shaped like raindrops filled with creamy cheese and chicken. How could I have lived so long and never tasted coxinhas?

After dinner, he'd light the fireplace, hold me close in our four-poster bed, and we'd talk about everything and nothing. Even though I begged and tried to seduce him, he refused to have sex with me till the bandages were off and the wounds healed. He wouldn't touch me in any sexual way, saying he couldn't start something and not finish it.

One Monday morning, he'd gotten up early, as he usually did, and came back to bed. He kissed me. "Mornin', babe."

"Mmm. Morning."

"Good news."

"Yeah?"

"You can take your bandages off today."

"I can? Does that mean we can do it?"

"Yes." He waggled his eyebrows.

"Let's do it now." I wrapped my arms around his neck and tugged, but he held back.

"Let's do our morning walk first."

What? Wait? Hadn't he been going crazy like me? "No. Let's do it before and after the walk. We have to make up for six lost weeks, and I'm aching for you."

He helped me stand and pulled me close. "I know. Me too, believe me, me too, but let's go walk."

"It's cold out there."

"Fresh air. Get your blood flowing. It's twenty degrees warmer here than in Boston."

He was right. I was being a wimp. "Okay. Let me get some warm clothes on."

He grinned.

————————

TORREZ HELD MY HAND as he had done every morning so far. I loved the way walking with him on the beach made me feel. Natural and easy. It's like his strength and joy came through our hands and lifted my heart too. I felt happy with him. The kind of happy that never leaves you. The kind of happy that changes your life so much, you can never believe you lived without it. I'd only met this man two months ago, yet he'd showered me with an ocean of love and experience in that time. If we packed this much into our first two months, I can only imagine how exciting our life would be together.

"Take off your shoes." He stopped near the water line for no apparent reason.

"No! Too cold."

"Life is too short for no. Say yes. Feel the cold. Prove you're alive."

Over the past few weeks, I'd discovered Torrez' philosophical side. At first I thought he was a meat and guns kind of guy, but over many long nights chatting in front of the fire, I found he was really smart and liked to analyze the world from an impartial observer's perspective. A few topics hit him too deep and caused him to stop talking. He wouldn't tell me any details about the Navy, his deployments as a SEAL, or what kind of things he had to do. He'd talk about the weather and living conditions. He went on and on about Dallas and his other brothers in arms, but whenever I asked him specifics, he'd shut down and change the topic. I don't know if he couldn't tell me or just chose not to. He focused on topics like "becoming your true self" and "seizing life."

"I don't need to freeze my tootsies to prove I'm alive." I answered his stupid request to go into the water now.

"Take off your shoes, roll up your pants, and feel the ocean on your feet. Trust me."

A reality check? Now? The bitter wind of January hit my feet as I took off my socks. I tried to think of his logic. You couldn't do this in Boston this time of year without risking losing a toe. That didn't mean we should do it here.

I squealed as he guided me into the whitewater of an approaching wave. It hit my ankles and pulled me in as it receded.

"Deeper," he said.

"No!"

"C'mon. You like it deeper. You're always begging me for it."

"Shut up." I smacked his shoulder and followed him deeper. He was right. The bite of the cold water did make me feel alive, but I could also feel alive in our warm bed with him making love to me.

A few steps in, he stopped and turned to me. The look in his eye stole my breath. The green turned to emerald, his smile held a secret, and his whole body was open to me, calling me closer.

And then he did something that shocked me.

He bent one knee and pushed it down into the water. His pants got wet, but he kept his eyes locked on mine.

"What're you doing?" I laughed.

His smile grew wider as he pulled a box from his pocket. He opened it and showed me a gold ring with a solitaire diamond.

I stepped back and sucked in a huge breath of salt air. Was he proposing? Now? To me? But—

He opened his mouth, and I thought I'd die if he asked me to marry him. This must be a joke. Why would he bring me out into the ocean to propose?

With a strong gust of wind, the ring slipped from his fingers and tumbled into the water!

"Shit." He dropped to both knees and fished around for it.

"Oh no!" I hit the water too, barely feeling the cold. We had to find that ring before the waves carried it away.

The longer we looked the wetter we got. At least a dozen waves came and went, and we didn't find the ring. He sat back on his ankles and sighed.

"We have to keep looking." I kept digging deeper in the sand with my nails. The holes I dug filled in again instantly.

"Let it go. I'll get you another ring," he said flippantly. Like he didn't just drop our future down the toilet.

"No." I fanned my hands out, crawling deeper into the surf. My fingers had gone numb.

He tugged on my arm, but I pulled back.

"You're shivering and your lips are turning blue. Give up."

"No! We have to find it. Never give up. Never!"

"Soraya." He stopped looking and stood still in the waves. I looked up and saw something pass in his eyes. He reached into his shirt pocket and pulled out another box. "That wasn't the real ring. This is your ring."

What? Fake ring? We lost a fake ring? "Are you pranking me right now?"

"I was before. Now I'm not."

What the hell was he talking about? This made no sense. "You didn't just drop a diamond ring into the Gulf of Mexico?"

"No. That one was a fake. Plastic. This one is real." He took my left hand and worked the ring on my shivering ring finger. "I want you to wear it and be my wife."

I yanked my hand away, making sure to push the ring all the way on. Didn't want to lose another one. "You big moron! You got me soaking wet, freezing cold and faked losing my wedding ring, and now you expect me to marry you?"

He grinned at me like I was being cute. "Not the response I was hoping for."

That made me even more angry. "Screw you!" I sloshed through the water back up to the shore. "Screw you and whatever bone-head horse you rode in on." His chuckle behind me reached my ear over the sounds of the wind and the waves. "It's not funny, you imbecile!"

He followed me down our private boardwalk, up the stairs, and into the living room. I kicked off my soaked sandals and stomped up the stairs to our bedroom, dripping ocean water on the floor as I went.

I peeled off my clothes and grabbed my silk robe from behind the door. "Go away, you big doofus!" I slid the robe on but it was far too thin to provide any warmth. It stuck to my skin like wet tissue paper. I looked up and his eyes drank me in just like they did that first morning when I was wearing a see-through nightie. My man was affected by my body. I liked that. I liked it a whole lot.

"Teimosa, listen to me." God, his soft voice was like a kiss. He looked delicious as he took my arms in his hands and forced me to face him. His wet clothes clung to every curve like fondant frosting on a cake. I stared at his pecs, mesmerized by the shadow and bump of his nipple under the fabric. The chill still stung my toes but my core heated.

"In boot camp, we line up nut to butt and sit in the current with our legs wrapped around the man in front of us." My gaze moved from his chest to his face. His eyes were patient, but begging me to hear him. I drilled my attention on his lips, which were also distracting, and tried to listen. He continued once he saw he had my attention. "The drill instructor laughs while our balls freeze off. He taunts us about being pussies needing to press our dicks to a man's ass to keep it from freezing off. We might sit there fifteen minutes, maybe an hour. Not one man gives a shit about the position or the DI's taunting. You know what they care about?"

"Getting the fuck out of there?"

"Yes. And also staying."

"Why?"

"The weakest men are the ones who drop out right before the end. The ones that make it are the men you want on your team. Because they'll survive when others fail. It's not about physical strength. It's about mental fortitude."

"What does that have to do with us?"

"This trip we're on ain't gonna be easy. We'll face storms, hurricanes. We'll get pummeled by forces out of our control. Sometimes we'll be sitting balls deep in frigid water. There will be times you'll want to give up and you think you can't make it. But I'll be there. You wrap your arms and legs around me and hold on for the ride." He pulled me in close and his heat sank into my heart. He kissed the top of my head. "Hang onto me.

I'll keep you warm. I got the mental strength, and I know you do too. Let me be the man you cling to when you're cold. We can be so strong together. Forever."

I rubbed my forehead against his hard chest. Damn Torrez. So smart and saying just what I needed to hear. "This you could have said without the demonstration."

His chest shook with his laughter. "Yeah, but look how hard your nipples are. Feel like rocks against my chest."

I smacked his shoulder. "Shut up, you numbskull."

He shook with laughter again.

His thumbs under my chin tilted my head to his and he kissed me. Salty, cold, divine. I opened for him and his heat invaded my mouth. We both dove deeper and groaned. Oh my god. I wanted him so bad.

I ended the kiss and pretended to be mad. "Fine. Give me the ring." I held out my hand palm up like a spoiled child.

"You're already wearing the ring." He turned my palm over and pointed to the giant rock propped there. Oh yeah, right. Well... I forgot.

I could not tear my eyes from the beauty I saw. A stunning princess-cut diamond beamed from the center like a billboard. Two square rubies graced either side of the massive diamond. Fine platinum bands held tiny ruby baguettes stacked horizontally next to each other in neat rows. It was the most stunning piece I'd ever seen. Modern and yet classic. A little loud and unique too. It screamed my style. Torrez knew me. He knew my tastes already. And any man who could pick out a ring like this for me was a keeper.

"You like it?"

"Of course I do. It's perfect."

"Good."

"I would've loved the simple ring too. The one you dropped in the ocean."

"I know you would, meu amor. And I absolutely love that about you. I know you don't give a shit about my money or jewels or whatever else material in this world. I know you love me for me."

"I do."

"That's why you'll be my wife."

"Okay."

I hated to mention it, but it needed to be said. "Should we uh.... I mean I'm technically still married to Yegor."

His eyes flashed with anger at the mention of his name. "He's dead."

"Oh my god. He is?"

"Pavel turned on him and fled."

Pavel? How odd. He was the most mild mannered of Ivan's three sons. I didn't even believe he wanted to marry Nariam.

"Nariam."

"What?"

"The girl they forced him to marry. We need to help her."

He stared at me for a long time, but didn't argue. "I'll talk to Rogan and Zook about going back for Nariam."

"Thank you."

"You set a wedding date. I'll plan around it. You want to wait?"

Absolutely not. I wanted to marry him as soon as possible. "I don't want to wait."

"Good. Get a dress. Get Cecelia a dress. Whatever you want. We can fly anywhere in the world. Have you been to Atlantic City?"

"No. And I'd love to go see it, but let's get married right here. On our deck. This home is so beautiful. I can't imagine a better place."

"Alright. And plan a honeymoon too."

"Oh, like where?"

"Anywhere you want. Rogan's stepdad is the Prime Minister of St. Amalie. You ever been there?"

"Is that in the Caribbean? It sounds familiar."

"Yep. White sand and warm days. Would love to see you lounging around in your bikini. Or naked."

"Oh, I'd love that."

"Then it's set." He kissed me again and my heart melted into his. My man, my love, my life.

My hands skimmed down his wide back and landed on his ass.

He planted a kiss on my lips and pulled away with a dashing grin. "Shower first. Then I'm taking your ass."

A zing of excitement ran from my heart to between my legs. "Okay."

"Got a platinum dildo for you. You'll be double stuffed. So full of me you won't know anything else."

Oh gosh. That sounded scary and wonderful at the same time. Just like everything with Torrez. "Okay," was my breathy reply.

He picked me up and carried me to the shower. We warmed our frozen toes. Standing next to Torrez' huge cock and rubbing soap all over him was an orgasmic experience. He ate me out as I gasped and screamed and held his head.

His kisses were slow and languid as he carried my relaxed body to the bed. He was taking his time even though we were both excited. He lay me down flat on my back and pushed my feet back so my legs opened to him. I was too far gone in the experience of extreme cold from the ocean and the heat from the shower to care what I looked like.

He took his time, making sure everything was good for me. And it was. I loved feeling so full and connecting with him on this intimate level.

We both came hard, sweating and grunting through it all. My god, he was right. I'd never leave him. Never.

He collapsed on me, breathing heavy. His arms supported most of his weight, but he gave me enough to feel safe and warm under him. I hugged him with my whole body. Legs, pussy, arms, even my head pressed closer. He groaned. He felt the love I sent him in that hug.

"Minha." Mine.

With his eyes closed, he trailed his fingers down my left arm and found my hand. He brought my wrist up between our faces and kissed my palm near my ring finger.

"Agora todos que cruzarem nosso caminho, saberão que você é minha."

"Oh God. That's gorgeous but I can't understand you."

He laughed and his smile made his already fabulous face even more spectacular. "It means *now everyone who crosses our path will know that you're mine.*"

I closed my eyes and let that wash through me. I was his. He was mine. We both had received a great gift. Gratitude and joy welled up in me and escaped through a tear from the corner of my eye.

He licked it away. "I will kiss your tears and drink your sorrow forever."

"Stop. I can't handle any more."

"I'll make you happy. You'll never feel lonely again. You'll never have to doubt me."

"I said stop!"

"Are you happy?"

"I'm so blissed out I can't see straight. I'm overwhelmed. I'm so full."

"Yes. Perfect."

We cuddled and kissed a little longer before he pulled out and removed the dildo. He tucked my back to his front and snuggled his nose by my ear. "I love you, Teimosa."

"I love you too, Torrez. Thank you for loving me."

"Forever."

Chapter 23

_{————}

T orrez

My wife's ring glinted in the cabin light of the plane. Two weeks alone with Soraya on St. Amalie was just what we needed after the stress of planning a wedding. We'd kept it simple. Just our closest friends. She'd pulled it off without a hitch. She looked stunning in her beachy wedding dress and planned all the details. She handled the entire event with grace, everyone had fun, and she said she felt fulfilled and satisfied, which made me happy.

The honeymoon, on the other hand, stressed her out. She agreed we should go to St. Amalie, but she couldn't settle on a resort. She felt overwhelmed by all the choices and gave up. I took over and planned the trip.

I lifted our joined hands and kissed her fingertips. "All good?"

She smiled and looked up from the travel magazine she'd been studying during the flight. "Yes. I'm nervous for some reason."

"New places are always a bit scary."

"I want to see this Poisson Bleu Cove." She pointed to a heart-shaped cove with clear water surrounded by tall black volcanic peaks.

"It's at the top of the list. You've mentioned it a few times. What is it about that place that intrigues you?"

"I don't know. The shape of the cove. And you can swim with manta rays. And the crystal blue water. It's all just calling to me."

"We'll be there in a few hours. Try to relax."

She didn't of course. She kept reading and re-reading the article about Poisson Bleu Cove.

"WHERE TO?" THE TAXI driver asked.

"The Pintaro Resort," I replied.

He nodded and pulled the taxi onto a narrow road that would take us up to the most exclusive resort on the island.

Thank you, Rogan and your prime minister of a stepdad, for booking us the coveted Treehouse Suite. We'd be up in the tops of the rainforest, with views of the volcanos and the beaches. The waiting list for the room was three years long, but Rogan got us in with less than a month's notice. My plan was to keep her naked and tied up in that room the entire two weeks. I suppose if she wanted to go sight seeing I could untie her for an afternoon.

I leaned back in my seat and let the island atmosphere hit me. I draped my arm around Soraya. She stiffened and stared out the window of the cab. Now, in the time I'd known my wife—apart from the first night in the hotel in Milton—I'd never felt her stiffen and pull away when I touched her. She always melted into me, welcoming me.

"Something wrong, babe?"

She rubbed her thumb and forefinger across her forehead. "It's just a headache."

"Get you some pain reliever as soon as we hit the resort."

"No." Her eyes cut to mine and something brewed there. Couldn't read it, but something was amiss. "Can we go to Poisson Bleu first?"

"Let's get settled in our room first, get you some Tylenol, christen the bed if you're feeling better."

"No. Let's go straight to Poisson Bleu Cove."

Okay. Definitely off. My girl never said no to sex.

"Alright." I raised my voice for the taxi driver. "Change of plans. Can you take us to Poisson Bleu Cove instead?"

He glanced over his shoulder at us. "It is about twenty minutes away."

"That's fine. Take us there."

He nodded again and pulled the car to the shoulder. One other car passed, and he pulled back out into traffic, this time heading the opposite direction.

When we arrived at the cove, Soraya's eyes were so wide, she wasn't blinking. She'd stopped making eye contact with me, stopped holding my hand, and her stare was far away.

"God, babe. What's going on?"

She shook her head slowly. "I need to see the manta rays at Poisson Bleu Cove."

"We're on our way."

She looked at me but didn't see me. "Are they still there? The manta rays?"

I caressed her cheek, trying to get her to come back to me. "Yes, they should be there. You saw them in the magazine, and it's the right season. You want to go in with the manta rays?"

She gasped and stared at me, pupils fully dilated. "Go in the water? With the manta rays? The water is blue."

"Yes, babe. The water is blue. Fuck. You're freaking me out."

I pulled her head to my chest and rubbed her temple with my palm. As if I could wipe away the thoughts messing with her head. Her heart beat like a hummingbird against my chest as we drove into the parking lot of the preserve. Her head popped up, and she craned her neck to see over the cliff down to the cove.

She jumped out of the cab and skidded on the sand, rushing to get to the path down. I tossed some cash at the cabbie and raced after her. "Soraya!"

Her feet slipped, and she fell on her ass, giving me a chance to catch up. I helped her to her feet and held her close. She stared at the part of the cove visible from our spot on the winding path. The sea air blew her hair into her face. She wrenched in my arms.

"Let me go. God! Let me go. No. They're not here!"

"What's not here? Have you been here before?"

We locked eyes. Yes, dammit. She'd been here before.

She took a breath and faked a calm demeanor. "Let me go," she said slowly.

I released her, and she took off running down the steep path. She stumbled but didn't fall. She ran across the white sand with her knees high. She struggled with the sand, but didn't give up.

She jumped into the water with her clothes on and ran toward a boat surrounded by snorkelers. I caught her then because I didn't know how she'd react if she actually saw a manta ray. She kept searching the water around us even though my arms held her immobile.

"They're harmless. They don't bite." She stared into the water, her chest heaving from the run.

"Manta rays don't bite," I answered.

"They don't sting you."

"No, babe. They won't." We were shoulder-deep in the warm water. Her gaze moved to Mount Pintaro and scanned around the beach. It wasn't too crowded. About thirty people on the beach, another ten snorkeling. "We can see the manta rays later. Let's go talk on the beach. Come to me."

Her lips turned down and her brows pulled together like a frightened child. "Run!" Soraya's yell startled the few people in the water near us. I let her go and she ran for the shore. I tackled her as soon as she reached the shoreline. She went ballistic. Screaming and thrashing under me. "Let me go!" Tears streamed down her face.

"Soraya. Come back to me. You're lost. It's me, babe. It's Torrez. You're safe. They won't sting you." I'm sure she didn't hear me. She was screaming and fighting too hard. Her eyes were closed. "Fuck." I needed to get through to her.

I placed my palms on either side of her head and kissed her. Pressed my lips to her wet, sandy lips and just kissed her. We rubbed awkwardly for a few seconds, and then she stilled.

When her eyes partially opened, she seemed to focus on me. "They'll take me."

"No one will take you. You're here with me. You're mine. You're safe. I won't let anyone take you." I pressed my whole body over hers, engulfing her in a cocoon of safety. And fuck me, fuck. It all became clear.

They took her. They took her from here. She wasn't adopted. She was stolen.

"Did someone take you from here? From your family?"

Her eyes locked on mine again. Yes, she was calming down and coming back to me.

Pain crinkled her face, and she tilted her chin to the left. I never wanted to see that look on her face again. An abducted child, scared and confused.

"They took you from your family. They took you to Veranistaad and told you you were adopted."

"Yes." She tucked her forehead to my chest and sobbed. "Yes. I remember now. I remember so much. I was afraid of the manta rays. My family went snorkeling with them, but I wandered off. Someone took me and carried me away. I was screaming..."

"I hear you. I get you're scared and confused. But listen to my voice because I'm gonna bring you back to right here and now. I got you out of Veranistaad and brought you here on our honeymoon. This is a different trip. You're an adult, you're married, and you're safe. I swear to fuck no one will take you. Understand?"

She nodded into my chest, but the tears didn't ebb. Her shoulders heaved with her sobs. I needed to get her out of here to someplace private. A lifeguard approached us. "Everything alright?"

"She's fine." I lifted her in my arms. She tucked her head and didn't look at the lifeguard.

"I can call an ambulance."

"No. She's just tired. I need a car. Is our taxi still there?" I carried her like a babe in my arms to the path.

"Let me run and check." The lifeguard took off up the path as I carried her. He ran back and skidded to a halt. "The taxi is there."

"Tell him to wait for us."

I followed him up the path running as fast as I could without hurting her.

———

HER BREATHING EVENED out within the first few minutes in the cab. I stroked her hair and continued to offer encouraging words in her ear. Told her I understood, and I'd help her through this.

I called ahead to the resort and told them to meet us at the taxi to check us in. I carried her up the stairs to our treehouse and lay her in the bed.

"Let me get you some water." I brought her a bottled water from the mini fridge.

She sat up and sipped it. Thank God, my Soraya's light had returned to her eyes. She still looked upset, but the worst had passed.

"You wanna talk about it?"

"I don't know how old I was. I can't remember everything. I get images. Scenes. Sometimes memories with no picture, just a feeling. I thought it was déjà vu, but when I saw the blue water and the snorkelers, I remembered. I was with my family. I left them and walked down the beach on my own. A man grabbed me. That's all I remember. I don't remember arriving in Veranistaad or who took me. I don't remember who told me I was adopted. I just always accepted it as a fact. I remember learning the language. I remember when they brought Cecelia and told me she was my adopted sister. Years are missing. But I'm sure I was on that beach with my family and that was the last time I saw them."

"Can you remember any names? Your name?"

"I don't know. The name Macy keeps coming to mind. I'm not sure if that was my name or my mom's. I don't remember if I had brothers and sisters. Atlanta. Why do I feel like I lived in Atlanta?"

"This is a lot to take in. Let's sleep tonight. Tomorrow we'll get you an appointment with someone to talk to. If they don't have a qualified therapist on the island, we'll fly home."

"What if I forget while I sleep?"

"I don't think you will. I think more memories are going to come to you." I held her in my arms. "You want to shower first?"

"No."

I grabbed a clean tee from my bag and slipped her wet clothes off, helping her into a new shirt.

"I don't want to cut our honeymoon short because I've had parts of my memory return."

"Okay. We'll find someone on the island to help you. If it's alright with you, I'd like to call Zook and talk to Cecelia to see what she remembers."

"Yes. I want to speak with her too."

"Sleep now. We'll call when you wake up."

"Okay."

I tucked her into my arms, kissed the top of her head. Her hand came up and caressed my abs and chest. She may have been absent-mindedly exploring, but she was driving me insane and my dick got hard.

"Torrez?"

"Yeah?"

"I can't sleep."

"I see that."

"It's technically our wedding night."

"You saying you want me to make love to you after all you've been through today?"

"Yes. To connect with you. Feel reality. Know I'm here with you."

"Are you sure?"

"Yes."

So I kissed her. Then I made it very clear her reality was here with me now. No way you could miss it.

———————

SORAYA CALLED CECELIA when we woke up. She cried as she retold the story of the cove and the manta rays and all the memories crashing down on her. She listened for a long time, sniffling. I left the room to give her some privacy.

Soraya was abducted and sold as a slave. I couldn't even imagine the shock she must be experiencing after thinking she was adopted all these years.

She sighed as she disconnected.

"Talking to her help?" I sat next to her on the bed.

"Yes."

"You wanna share with me? I get it if it's between you two, but I'm here to listen if you need an ear."

"It was good. The truth is out between us now. She'd kept her history from me all these years, and I'd forgotten my past." She blew her nose into a tissue. She still looked gorgeous, red nose and all.

"Hey, there's no shame here. You're both victims. You did nothing to deserve this."

"Logically I know that. Inside I feel shame. I forgot everything?"

"You probably blocked it out. Too painful. Maybe your subconscious knew you were safe with me and let the memories surface."

"Yes. Your love opened the floodgates."

I kissed her. "Pleased as fuck I got to be part of this."

She smiled. "I'm also ashamed I didn't escape sooner. I was in the States for college. I could've left if I'd just been brave, but Cage..."

"The one who hit you?"

"Yes."

"If I ever see that dude, he's gonna be limping home holding his teeth in his hands."

She stared at me without blinking.

"Okay. What about Cage?"

"When he hit me, he squashed all my dreams. I left and went home believing no one would ever save me. Cecelia did too. We both fled like cowards."

"Hey, when life hits us with a painful blow, our instinct is to run. Shoot, I ran when I first realized you meant something special to me. I ran from Greco. The important part is we both stopped running."

"Yeah."

"Whatever comes our way. No matter what memories assault you, I'm here. We'll face it together." I kissed her a long time, until her shoulders relaxed and the sadness left her eyes. Needed to fuck her again, but had one question first.

"Considering this is all new to you, I'm going to give you some time. But I think we should share this info with Rogan when you're ready."

"Why?"

"Couple reasons. One, to see if Rogan made any inroads bringing Ivan to justice. And two, Rogan's good at finding people."

"So?"

"Maybe he could find your parents."

Her eyes snapped wide. "I don't know. It's been so long. I feel terrible for not remembering. It would be so difficult for everyone." Tears welled in her eyes, and her lips pressed together. "Do you think they'd want me back?" The despair of an abandoned child returned to her beautiful face. Yegor died for placing that look there. His fucked up father was next on my list. No more waiting for indictments or hits. I'd handle the king the same way I handled the son. Deadly stealth.

"Million bucks they're waiting for the day you come back to them. Parents never give up hope. They'll welcome you with open arms. Do anything they can to try to make up for the lost time. But I gotta say it bothers me you'd ask that question.

Cecelia's parents, another story, they sold her. Losers don't deserve to have her in their lives. But you were abducted. You didn't do anything wrong. They won't blame you for it. And you shouldn't blame yourself."

"But I forgot them."

"They'll understand."

"Okay then. Yes. If we could find them, I'd like to try."

"Let's let it sit for a while. Get you talking to a therapist to help you process all the memories. When you're ready, we'll hire Rogan to start looking for them."

"Alright. And I'd like to visit Cecelia before we go back to Texas."

"We can do that."

"Thank you."

"Anything for you, babe. I swear anything for you."

———

TEN MONTHS LATER, TORREZ was in the kitchen cooking, and I was binge watching a show about a motorcycle gang.

A message came through on my phone.

Cecelia: Recognize anyone in this picture?

She sent a picture of several actors on a stage. Each of them dressed like Roman warriors. One of the men stood out as bigger, more casual, and oh my god, that was Falcon.

My lips sputtered.

Me: OMFG! Is that Falcon?

She had a date with Zook to see the opera in New York. What the heck was Falcon doing up on the stage?

Cecelia: I think it is!

She and Zook had met Falcon at Rogan's Christmas party. She didn't know him as well as I did, but Falcon made a big first impression.

Me: I cannot believe what I'm seeing.

I added a crying sideways laughing emoji.

Cecelia: I know!

I clicked on the picture and zoomed in on him. He was wearing nude tights and looked like he'd rather have pins shoved under his fingernails than stand on that stage.

Me: He's wearing tights!

Cecelia: I know. I can't stop laughing. #putaforkinme

Another sputter burst from my lips. He looked so awkward and out of place. What the heck?

Torrez walked out of the kitchen holding a dishtowel. "What's funny?"

"What does puta mean?" I asked him.

His eyebrows drew up. "It means fuck usually. Or bitch. Why?"

I scrunched my eyes to make sure I was reading the text correctly. That didn't sound like a word Cecelia would use. Plus she didn't even speak Spanish. "Puta for Kinme. Who is Kinme?"

"Let me see that." He took my phone, read the text, and rolled his eyes. "It's a hashtag. No spaces between the words." He threw his head back and laughed.

"I know that, but this one is in Spanish."

His laugh bellowed through the room. "It's put a fork in me."

"Put a fork in me?" I stared at the hashtag. What was he laughing at?

"Like I'm done. Put a fork in me."

I stared at it long enough and I finally got it. "Oh. I see it now."

He laughed for a good five minutes more as he worked in the kitchen.

"Shut up." I was learning about social media, but I didn't have any personal profiles up for safety reasons. I walked into the kitchen and set my phone on the counter. "I know what a hashtag is. I just thought it was in Spanish."

His hand held his stomach as he doubled forward.

"Good thing you're so damn gorgeous when you laugh or I'd be pissed at you."

A few more chuckles ran through him. "Love you, babe." He picked up my phone and did a double take. He tapped on the picture of Falcon. "What the hell? Oh shit. That is classic. Classic. Send me that picture. I'm using it as leverage."

As I was forwarding it to him, his phone rang.

He listened quietly for a long time. "Thanks," was all he said before he disconnected.

"Who was that?"

"Rogan."

"And all you said was thanks? What did he say?"

He turned off the stove and walked over to me. His arms circled me and his eyes grew serious. "He has a lead on a possible match for your family."

My heart lurched. "He does?"

"Atlanta. Macy and Edward Abernathy." He waited for my reaction.

Abernathy. Abernathy. Yes, I knew that name. I could taste it. I could smell it.

"Yes. I think. Yes. That sounds... right."

The corners of his mouth turned up. "Go pack. We're going to Atlanta."

"We are?" My heart fluttered. "Okay, but can we fly? No road trips?" A road trip would take far too long and now that I'd found them, possibly, I wanted to get there the fastest way.

He chuckled and kissed my nose. "We can fly."

Chapter 24

Five years later

The BRX came to Atlanta five years after we got hitched. Drew made his way into the shoot. My gut churned knowing it was not a matter of if you'd get hurt riding a bull, it was how bad.

The announcer called him out as the grandson of Adriano Durango Lavonte. Then they added a spotlight on me.

"Drew's father is with us tonight. Tauro Bravo Lavonte was a hell of a rider in his day. Take note, folks. You're looking at a family of warriors. From a founding father to a grandson, the bull runs in their blood. They live and die by the bull. The BRX legacies."

I waved, proud as shit of my boy, and finally accepting the acknowledgment I had a good run in my day. Also took in the applause for my dad's memory. Hard as nails, but still a brave man who did a good thing for the sport of rodeo and made me the man I am today. Not to mention the money from the BRX was incredible.

The lights went back to Drew alone on the bull, spotlighting him as he deserved. He shined so much more than me or my dad ever did. He had god-given talent, he had sprawl, and he worked his ass off to get here tonight.

Directly in front of Soraya and I, Peyton bit her nails and peered at the ring while on her tiptoes. She attended all his shows when she could make it work with her schedule at Hale. The way she loved her brother and he loved her, that was priceless. Soraya held our twins close on either side. Our four-year-old boy, Levi, had my eyes. Our girl, Lola, had her smile and her hair. Those kids were like our love, parts of her and parts of me twisted together in a gorgeous song, the way it was meant to be. Man, I loved being a dad.

Jackie and Duffy didn't usually come to Drew's shows, but they came to this one because he had the potential to win his fourth world championship. They sat directly in front of Peyton, but didn't turn around and talk to us, which was fine by me. We'd come to a resolution of tolerance around each other that involved minimal conversation, only what was necessary to discuss the kids. I did not give a shit about her personal life, and she'd grown wise enough to stay out of mine.

Soraya's biological parents stood next to her. Macy and Edward Abernathy had stayed in Atlanta, not wanting to leave in case Soraya ever came looking for them. And when she did, whoa boy, that was a heart-wrenching day for her. Memories flooded her brain. The tears flowed for hours. Lots of hugging and catching up on a lifetime of missed memories.

Her bio parents took Peyton, Drew, and the twins into their hearts, not differentiating where the DNA came from. We'd become an interwoven family. We took trips like this in the RV, following Drew on the BRX circuit. Just like I'd done as a kid with my parents. Only this time was different. This time

I praised my kid after every ride. This time there was no pressure on me to be Tauro Bravo. The pressure was on Drew, but he loved the challenge and the attention. After eight rounds, he was tied for first and his last round was up next.

I wrapped my arm around Soraya's neck and kissed her temple.

Being Soraya's husband was better than I'd ever imagined. Love so deep, it was part of me. Great sex. Fun times whenever we were together and wanting to get back to her any time I had to leave her. Watching her become a mother and giving those kids all the closeness and caring she missed out on growing up.

I lucked out. But most of all, it was her respect for me. She never looked at me like I was a criminal. The beauty of being loved unconditionally. She forgave all the shit from my past and loved me as the man I was now.

Drew gave the signal. The handlers pulled the gate open, and the bull burst out. He gave Drew a hell of a ride. Kicking all four off the ground at once, twisting left and right, throwing crazy steep back angles. As the eight seconds ticked by, the anticipation of the crowd exploded. Drew rode with his unique flare. My boy had fluid style. All the rodeo girls told him that too, but he never got a big head. He knew humility was important in bull riding. You respect the bull, you stay alive. Never be bigger than the bull.

The crowd gasped. I held my breath as he hit the ground and the bull bucked. The bull fighters swept him out of the way and distracted the bull. He bucked his way all the way back into the pen.

He made it. An awesome ride. No injuries. A few tense moments passed as we all waited for the score for him and his bull.

Holy shit. Ninety-five! "Ninety-five!" The announcer echoed the score on the screen. The crowd went nuts! To get a ninety was a huge feat. Ninety would have won him the competition, but ninety-five sent him into another galaxy.

Number one bull rider in the world four times in four years. He'd won this and two other grand championships this year, leaving both mine and my dad's records in the dust.

Soraya jumped into my arms and wrapped her legs around my waist. We spun around and kissed, wet and deep. This was ours. Our family. Our destiny. Free and clear. We'd found it. We'd fought hard for it, and the victory was sweet.

Want More?

———

Sign up to Bex Dane's VIP reader team and receive exclusive Men of Siege bonus content including;

- Free Books

- Deleted scenes

- Secrets no one else knows

- Advanced Reader Copies and first look at cover reveals

Give me more[1]!

———

1. https://bexdane.com/

Made in the USA
Middletown, DE
02 March 2020

85693517R00170